# TILTED SKY

# TILTED SKY

Yao Emei

Translated by Kelly Zhang

LEVINE QUERIDO

Montclair | Amsterdam | Hoboken

This is an Em Querido book
Published by Levine Querido

LEVINE QUERIDO

www.levinequerido.com • info@levinequerido.com
Levine Querido is distributed by Chronicle Books, LLC
Text copyright © 2010 by Yao Emei
Translation copyright © 2024 by Kelly Zhang
Originally published as 倾斜的天空 by China Children's Press & Publication Group
(CCPPG)
Library of Congress Control Number: 2023940115
ISBN 978-1-64614-383-2
Printed and bound in China

Published in May 2024
First Printing

## ☼ Chapter 1

### Sunlight Splashed in Through the Window

Sunlight splashed in through the window. I woke up with a start and jumped out of bed. Today was my first day going back to school, and I didn't want to be late.

Actually, the fall semester officially kicked off a week ago. I was supposed to be in the sixth grade. But from the time I filled in my registration forms until now, I'd been stranded at home. To the outside world, I pretended like I didn't care, but deep down, I was becoming more restless.

Hei Jian didn't save up enough money to pay my school fees, again. It wasn't entirely his fault. I mean, nobody wants to be poor if they have a choice, right? The problem was, Hei Jian would never willingly admit that he was utterly broke.

According to Hei Jian, the world tries to divide people into two camps: the "poor" and the "rich," when they're actually two sides of the same coin. He says it's like a game of heads or tails. When you toss a coin, you might land on the poor side first. Toss it again, you might land on the rich side. Or here's another way to see it: "rich" and "poor" are like a pair of guards that change posts every few hours. But that's just Hei Jian's belief. I'm not so sure that's how things really work— that everyone's got the exact same chances.

Sometimes I couldn't resist ruffling Hei Jian's feathers. I would say, "You've been waiting on the poor side for so long. Why hasn't anyone rich come to change posts with you?"

To my surprise, the last time I challenged him on it, instead of getting upset like he usually would, Hei Jian just chuckled.

"My boy, it's too early to tell whether I'm poor or rich. One thing I've learned is that fortune is fickle—it will not allow people to stay rich or poor forever. So be patient, my boy. You'll see, my fortune is about to turn."

I told Hei Jian that in my mind, things were quite straightforward: if a person never has enough money to pay for important stuff like food and school . . . he's definitely poor.

"Who knows, let's hope that one day a bag of cash will drop from the sky and land right in my lap!" Hei Jian laughed loudly. "But just remember what I've always told you: don't give up, and never lose hope. Because anything can happen tomorrow." Hei Jian was so convinced of his brilliant, promising future that even I believed him sometimes.

Whenever Hei Jian spoke to me up close, I couldn't help turning my head away. His stomach was almost always empty, and, if a person hasn't eaten in a while, his breath starts to smell gross. I knew this from personal experience.

Yesterday morning, after Hei Jian had gotten up, he stood in front of the bathroom mirror and slicked down his long, messy hair. Then he bent over to put on his trusty old army boots. Hei Jian considered himself a "man's man." Even when he hadn't eaten all day, he still walked around with energy and stride. On those impossibly hot and humid summer afternoons, when one could barely breathe, Hei Jian still wore his bulky boots. People called him "cool" or "hip." But only I knew the truth: besides his boots, the only other shoes he owned were a pair of flip-flops.

Hei Jian is my dad, but he doesn't want me to call him "Dad." He prefers to be called "Hei Jian," which means "black keys," like the keys on a piano. Hei Jian is not his real name though. His real name is . . . never mind. It's super boring anyway—just forget it.

Anyhow, like I was saying, after Hei Jian had smoothed out his hair and laced up his boots, he ordered me to pack my schoolbag. "We're going to walk to your school together, first thing tomorrow morning."

Actually, I had already packed my schoolbag the week before. But since he'd issued a command, I had to obey. I repacked my bag. That was yesterday morning.

Last night, Hei Jian came home late as usual. Stomping across the bottom of the stairs, he'd hollered, "Bai Jian! Bai Jian!!!"

Oh right: "Bai Jian" is *my* name. It means "white keys," like on a piano. I don't know why he had chosen such an odd name for me. It made everyone think that my family name is "Bai" and his family name is "Hei."

As soon as I opened the door for him, the smell of booze instantly ambushed me. Hei Jian wrapped me inside a giant hug and kissed me on the face. He really only gave me hugs or kisses when he was drunk. Then he mumbled something about how I was the only family he's got in the world.

He was in good spirits.

"Ah, Bai Jian! My boy, my dear lad. Just you wait! We'll go visit your school tomorrow. I've got the money now. And right in the nick of time! Let me tell you—we're *not* poor! I can always make more money when we need it. Look! See this?" He pulled out a thick, tan-brown envelope from his coat pocket and slammed it on the table. A wad of pink one hundred yuan bills spilled from its throat.

To be clear, I'm not some kind of money-hungry kid. Most of the time, I couldn't care less about money. But in this case, having access to some funds meant I could go back to school, so I wasn't about to say no.

Hei Jian went on to tell me the whole story. Apparently, earlier in the day, he'd been sitting in his office, glaring at the old dial phone on his desk while racking his brain over how to get me my school money. (By the way, he was working now as an art director for a small advertising agency.) Maybe the phone didn't like being stared at like that, because it began to ring. He grabbed the handset and shoved it against his ear. It was a client who wanted him to design a commercial to promote their company's products. He immediately asked for a down payment.

When he got to that part of the story, my heart began to hop giddily inside my chest, but I kept my face calm and cool. "Nice," I replied nonchalantly. "Maybe from now on I should go stare at a phone too if I have nothing to do? Who knows, money may start to rain down on me!"

Hei Jian cuffed me on the back of the head. "Hey buddy, don't you play smart ass with me!"

Hei Jian likes to drink when he's happy. So, although he couldn't even walk straight anymore, he made me go fetch him another bottle of beer. He likes to drink while watching soccer on TV too. When his favorite team or player scores, he either pulls me out of bed and tosses me into the air, or cheerfully pinches my bum. If someone makes a bad pass or misses a goal, he gets so upset, he starts to hurl beer bottles at the wall. The first time he did that, I got so scared I almost peed my pants.

I knew it was going to be a long, sleepless night. But the thought of heading back to school the following morning lightened my mood.

After he drank the night away, Hei Jian passed out on the couch.

When I woke up this morning, I crouched down next to the couch but dared not disturb him. Hei Jian hates getting woken up from his rest, and right now, with his head laid across a pillow, he was sleeping like a log. Tufts of his long hair had knotted into a tangled nest, making him look like that haggard beggar always hanging out on Liberation Street.

After watching for a while and seeing zero sign of him stirring, I decided to go brush my teeth. On the way to the bathroom,

I deliberately made a series of loud noises. My idea was that even if I "accidentally" woke him up, I would be safely out of reach.

Sure enough, Hei Jian started rustling on the couch and, finally, woke up. Then he began to yell angrily. "Bai Jian! What the hell are you doing?! Be quiet!!!"

"Today's my first day back to school," I replied from inside the bathroom.

After a long pause, he groaned and got up. "Okay, so why are you still bumming around? Hurry up and get ready. Let's go!"

When we had finally gotten out of the door, Hei Jian led me down an unfamiliar path, in the complete opposite direction of my school. Confused, I stopped in my tracks and refused to cross the street. Hei Jian wrapped his arm around my shoulders and announced, "We're not going back to that old school of yours. I've signed you up for a different school this year. A boarding school, my boy. Nice and expensive—the kind of school where all the rich kids go."

I couldn't understand why he would do this to me, without even asking. I'd thought I was heading back to my old school—to my friends. I didn't want to go to a new school and meet a bunch of strangers! But I was too chicken to protest to his face then and there, so I kept my mouth shut. I tried to convince myself that it was better to have a school to go to rather than no school at all. Right?

Hei Jian shoved me along. I felt his slim, bony fingers poke the back of my neck like the cold barrel of a pistol. Things seemed to be happening so quickly and totally out of the blue. Everything was a command, to be obeyed and not questioned. I glared at him and fumed in my head. *How would you like it if I treat you this way when you're old and frail?*

"Hey boy," he said, "don't look at me like that. I've got my reasons. I can't keep myself chained to you forever." My slow walking speed must have really irritated him. He swooped up from behind me, then dragged me along as if pulling a puppet by its strings, forcing me to keep pace.

"Don't you see? If I don't go hang out with the right people, I won't succeed. And if I don't succeed, you won't have a comfortable life. And when I'm away, who's going to take care of you? Cook for you? Wash your dirty laundry? That's one of the perks of being in a boarding school—there's always someone around to help you out. You're going to be pampered like royalty. Just think about it: a poor kid, living like a prince! I couldn't even have dreamed of that when I was a kid."

Not for the first time, I answered, "Then why don't you just get me a mom? A mother can do all those things you mentioned. Besides, every kid I know has one. Why can't I have one too?"

"Foolish!" Hei Jian snorted. "I should be tied down to a woman just because you want a mom? Why do I have to sacrifice so much for you? We all deserve to live our own lives. And since we are friends— heck, best buddies—let's not act selfish and drag each other down, okay?"

I hesitated for a moment, then decided to speak up a little more. "But I *did* have a mom once, before you lost her. You took her away from me, Hei Jian. YOU are the truly selfish one here."

"Nonsense!" he snapped. "I didn't lose her. She left by herself!"

I liked to mess with his head sometimes. I found it kind of fun, like playing with math puzzles. One good thing about having a dad like Hei Jian is that you can speak your mind. You can talk to him about almost any subject under the sun and not worry about him getting offended—at least not for a while.

But I was still unsure about the whole boarding school thing. After all, my situation was probably very different from those of the other students. My mom was not around; I only had Hei Jian. And he was constantly trying to get rid of me.

When I was younger, Hei Jian would often lock me inside our place and go out for an entire day. After he had returned late at night, just when I thought he was finally ready for bed, someone would invite him out for a midnight snack.

So one night, I snuck out and followed him. I shut the front door behind me and whistled breezily, trotting down the street right behind him. Not long after, he bumped into a woman he knew, probably the one who asked him out. Thank goodness he slowed down as they walked together side by side, otherwise I wouldn't have been able to catch up. They got on a bus. Just as the bus door was about to close, I hopped on too. The bus driver plus nearly an entire busload of passengers stared at me, looking surprised and confused. When Hei Jian spotted me, he glared at me without saying a word. His face was dark and gloomy, his jaw tightly clenched. He looked *pissed*.

At the next stop, Hei Jian dragged me off the bus. That lady friend of his looked quite bummed. She waved bye to him through the window as the bus pulled away, and he waved back. Then he turned around and gave me a giant kick in the ass with his boot, sending me flying through the air like a frog. But to me, the pain of physical punishment was nothing compared to the stress I'd endured staying home alone.

Sometimes I would overhear our neighbors murmuring that if Hei Jian ditched me, I would be out on the streets mingling with a horde of beggars soon enough. We would swarm around pedestrians and cling to their trousers so tightly and desperately, they'd be forced to cough up some change.

I've always had this uneasy feeling that sooner or later, Hei Jian would indeed abandon me. I just hadn't expected that day to arrive so quickly. He used to tell me that instead of hanging around him, I should just go and pretend to be an orphan. Because an orphaned boy as handsome and charming as me would have no problem getting scooped up by some nice and well-to-do adoptive parents, ushered into a fancy new house, and set upon the path to a bright future. With this whole boarding school thing, he had finally found the perfect plan.

According to Hei Jian, the people at the boarding school would take care of all my needs. They would do everything he did for me, plus other things he didn't always do—like giving me nutritious meals and a nice bed to sleep on every night. The school was to become my new home basically. Hei Jian wouldn't have to worry about me starving or looking too scruffy or freezing to death anymore. In fact, he'd probably never need to think about me again. I would be gently and quietly erased from his life, like a teacher erasing words from a blackboard.

I started to feel very worried about my future. A future without Hei Jian.

Maybe I should have died as a baby eleven years ago. They told me that back when I was just eight months old, my mom had asked Hei Jian, "When are you going to marry me?"

To which he replied, "I'm not ready to get married yet."

Hei Jian was still in college back then. When his girlfriend at the time got pregnant and gave birth to their baby, he was forced to drop out from this prestigious film academy—his dream school. It was as if a thick, dark cloud had suddenly appeared out of nowhere and pulled his bright, sunny future into its clutches.

After dropping out of college, Hei Jian didn't go to find work right away. He didn't want to become a welder or some other kind of lowly laborer slogging away in a rundown, state-owned factory. At least, that's what he told my mom as the reason why he couldn't marry her.

So, that night—when I was barely eight months old—she left with her little suitcase in hand and never returned.

Maybe God didn't want me to have a mom. Since Hei Jian never owned a single picture of my mom, I didn't even know what she looked like.

Isn't it awful? To think that one day my mom might be standing at the corner of a street, glancing over at me, and I wouldn't even know it. Whenever I thought about that scenario happening in real life, I would get super upset. It just felt so frustrating and unfair!

More than once, I played out this scene in my head: a fashionably-dressed young woman strolls down the street, looking this way and that. I follow her quietly and stealthily for a while. Then, I edge up to her and gently tap her on the shoulder. She spins around and stares at me, seemingly surprised. Finally, I can see her face up close—a face that radiates natural beauty. Since I'm extremely handsome and Hei Jian looks merely passable, according to the laws of genetics, she would be the nicer-looking parent. But she's also rather rude. She tries to shove me away with her arm as she mutters, "Who are you? Why did you bump into me?"

I keep staring at her, until a spark of recognition enters her eyes.

My nainai used to tell me that people who are related by blood will always find each other at the end of the road. Because there is a secret thread binding them together that's invisible to everyone else in the world.

It's now her turn to stare at me. Slowly, she draws closer to me and reaches out with trembling hands. "Can I touch your face?" she asks.

"No." I glare at her. "No way!"

Then I turn and walk away with my head held high.

My mom simply stands there, her feet frozen in place. Or else she slowly collapses to the ground, like in one of those slo-mo movie scenes. She stares at my back intensely and longingly, then bursts into tears on the curb as a curious crowd of passersby gather around her . . .

I don't feel bad for her at all. She deserves it, just and fair. Because on countless nights since I was a baby, I have lain awake alone in bed, staring up at the moon. I would think about my friends and how all their moms would come to school to pick them up. I would keep thinking until tears welled into my eyes and spilled down my face.

Why should I be the only one crying? Why shouldn't she cry too?

In fact, I would feel quite happy and smug watching her bawl her eyes out one day. But this was all in my imagination. The reality was, I didn't know where she was or what she looked like, let alone whether or not she would cry if she saw me on the street.

·☽· **Chapter 2**

It was an Exhausting Morning

It was an exhausting morning. Hei Jian took me to the boarding school, a small building standing near the bank of a river, a long walk from our apartment. I don't like rivers.

I had no clue what Hei Jian planned to do after he dropped me off at school, but during our walk there, he kept reminding me that I'm not an average kid. That I'm brilliant, extraordinary. And that one day, the world would come to know my brilliance.

Hei Jian loves movies. That's why he tried so hard to get into that famous film academy. But because of my untimely birth, and because my grandparents died one after the other within a short few years, he had to drop out of college. His youthful dreams and hopes burst like colorful bubbles under the sun. I used to blame myself for being a burden—a roadblock on his path to success. But one day, I stopped beating myself up when I realized that none of it was my fault. It's not like I was ever given the choice of whether to be born, and I certainly didn't have the power to direct his future.

Hei Jian had done this to himself with his recklessness and impatience. He should have waited until he had at least graduated from college before fathering a child. Heck, so many smart and accomplished people in this world have waited until their hair turned grey before having kids. Why couldn't he prioritize? Why did he have to do things without a plan? Anyway, even if I had somehow interfered with his life's goals, he totally deserved it.

After dropping out of college halfway through, Hei Jian spent his days putting up movie posters in his room and staring at them. Eventually, he started to call himself a director. "Go bring two bottles of beer for Director Hei!" he would command me. Or, "Come over here and give Director Hei a back massage!" His friends also began to call him Director Hei. Jokingly, of course. I could hear the mockery in their voices. But Hei Jian didn't seem to mind.

Hei Jian eventually found work as an art director for an advertising company. But within days of starting his new job, he was already bored working with the people there. He got reprimanded for "not being a good team player," so he quickly jumped ship to a different company. He didn't stay long at that company either. Since then, he has always been hopping from one place to the next. And every time he switches jobs, he changes his business card. He would spend an entire day or two mulling over his new job title and brainstorming a cool new design for the card. After all, an art director has to be creative and original, right?

The art-directing jobs he took on didn't improve his financial situation though. He still lived from paycheck to paycheck. His cell phone was always getting disconnected because he couldn't pay his phone bills on time. And time and time again, he would suddenly find himself without even a coin left in his pockets. We were often stuck eating instant noodles for every meal until he got paid. Then, as soon as he got his hands on more money, it'd be gone again in the blink of an eye. Like this time. I had been forced to postpone starting school for an entire week because Hei Jian ran out of money. And knowing him, it certainly wouldn't be the last time that something like this happens.

The boarding school he picked out for me prided itself on being an "artsy" school, so each student had to demonstrate some kind of artistic talent to be accepted. When we got to the main office, the head teacher asked me what my artistic talent was, and Hei Jian jumped in to answer for me: acting. Then he nudged me. "Hey kid, why don't you perform something for your teacher."

When I was very young, probably not long after Hei Jian had dropped out of college, Hei Jian would try to relive his dream of being a film student. He would chant folk rhymes and tongue twisters all day long to practice his articulation skills:

*"Seven hundred soldiers, shoulder to shoulder,*
*"Tumbled down the hills up north;*
*"On and on stretched the stretchers when*
*"Bombs and bullets began booming forth . . ."*

When he got bored of sitting around the house and talking to himself, he would teach me how to recite this rhyme. As a little kid, I thought it sounded funny, so I learned it. Ever since then, Hei Jian has asked me to perform the rhyme in front of random people. And each time, I hoped and prayed that it would be the last time. Now he was making me recite it again.

I stood there in the head teacher's office in silent, sulky protest, refusing to obey his command. Luckily, the teacher interjected by saying that unfortunately, the school didn't offer any acting classes— they only had music, dance, visual art, and voice classes. She suggested that I join the voice class, since I seemed to have a nicely timbered voice.

"Put him in whatever class you want," Hei Jian replied. "It doesn't matter, he's not going to be a professional artist. We're just looking for some quality education."

Hei Jian has never been an agreeable person. I think he went along with things today mainly because he was in a hurry to leave. Because as soon as we had walked into the school, he mentioned that he was traveling out of town soon, and that he planned to visit me once a month.

The head teacher went on to explain that students are expected to go home weekly on Friday afternoon and return to school on Sunday night. Hei Jian simply replied, "Okay."

After we had finished signing all the forms, I asked Hei Jian where I should go on weekends. "Go to Jing's place," he said. "I've already asked her. She'll come pick you up on Friday."

Jing is Hei Jian's ex-girlfriend. The three of us had spent a good amount of time together up until a few months ago. As a couple, they didn't seem to have gotten along all that well. They were always fighting and yelling and trying to break up. I still remember the day when Jing left, about six months ago. She had packed all her belongings into a nylon bag.

Without Jing around, our place instantly turned empty and dull—like a once-flourishing peach tree that suddenly gave up all its branches, leaves, and fruits. I had no idea where she'd gone to live. I'd have seen very little of her since then.

Jing is a very nice person. And she has always been extra kind to me. Whenever she spotted a children's clothing shop or toy store while we strolled down a street together, she would go in and buy something for me. Almost all the clothes I owned were gifts from her. She liked to search for new recipes and cook for us too.

"Bai Jian, you make me feel like a mom, and I really enjoy that feeling," Jing would say to me.

I haven't worn any new clothes since Jing moved out. Nor eaten any good food. Whenever Hei Jian has money to spare, he buys us fast food or large cases of those instant noodles. When he gets home at the end of the day, we would soak the noodles in hot water for a few minutes before eating them for dinner. If he hadn't returned home by the time I got hungry, I would open a packet of dry noodles, break them into smaller chunks, and snack on those.

Hei Jian used to call Jing his "wifey" and sometimes "big sis." (Jing is a bit older than Hei Jian.) I, on the other hand, would simply call her Jing, because she didn't like to be called "auntie" or "Auntie Jing." She thought the title "auntie" was too generic and boring—practically all the women in her age group are called "aunties" by little kids.

Even after their latest breakup, Hei Jian still called Jing his wife and big sis whenever he saw her. Before Jing, Hei Jian had many other girlfriends, and none of them stayed around for very long. That's probably because Hei Jian likes to beat people up. Almost every girlfriend he's had got beaten up at some point.

Jing moved out soon after he beat her up badly. That day, I saw him grab her hair and slam her head against the wall and choke her until a gurgling sound sputtered out of her throat. Strangely enough, they made up the very next day. I saw Jing smiling in the kitchen as she made breakfast for us, and Hei Jian was calling her "big sis" and "wifey" left and right.

But a few days later, Jing moved out, quietly and permanently. After Jing's departure, Hei Jian went through a rough patch. For days on end, he didn't eat anything until noon. And he stayed out even later at night, way past most people's bedtimes.

One night, Hei Jian went out for dinner super late, and when he returned, he drunkenly called Jing and chatted with her until his phone battery got so hot it scorched his ear. Then, he kept on crying and sobbing over the phone.

I once heard someone say about Hei Jian, "He was born a deadbeat, and he will stay one for the rest of his life."

Of course, I was mad when people made that sort of a comment about him. It's not nice. But to be honest, what they said wasn't completely false. At my old school, I met a lot of my classmates' parents, and none of them acted like Hei Jian and his girlfriends. They didn't fight all the time and make a clean, orderly room look like the apocalypse had just landed inside. Nor did they lock their lips and French-kiss in front of their kids. Nor did they share long and passionate hugs in the middle of a busy road, blocking the flow of traffic and making several lanes of cars blast their horns angrily at them—so embarrassing!

I adored my grandma. But sadly, Nainai passed away when I was barely five years old. Nainai seemed to know that she was going to die soon, because before she became too ill, she went around asking people to adopt me. She was quite worried that once she was gone, my living situation would become much harsher.

A nice couple *did* want to adopt me. They had already collected my things, and were about to take me out of Nainai's house when Hei Jian stormed in. He yelled at them and chased them away. Then Hei Jian started to yell at Nainai too.

"I've found him a good family, and people who will do a much better job at raising him than you," Nainai replied simply. "I want to make sure that my grandson will be well taken care of; that his stomach will not be filled one day and empty the next."

"So you only judge people by how much money they have?! How heartless of you! And how foolish, to trust those strangers so blindly!" Hei Jian hugged me tightly and wept as he told me how he was also adopted, and how he didn't want me to repeat his hard life.

His words must have broken Nainai's heart, because Nainai shouted, "You are the truly heartless one in this house! How have I brought you up all these years? Did I treat you badly? When I swaddled you in my arms and carried you out of the hospital, I couldn't have *imagined* all the pain and suffering I would have to overcome to raise you. But even to this day, you still only think about your birth parents. I may as well have raised a dog. A dog would at least wag its tail at its owner. Without me, you'd be stuck shoveling dirt in the countryside!"

Nainai's words stabbed Hei Jian where it hurt too, so he struck back with even more angry, hurtful words. And not long after their big fight, Nainai died.

It was said that my birth had caused great strife between the two sides of my family. My mom's side of the family despises Hei Jian and his family. To this day, they've never acknowledged me or Hei Jian. Only Nainai loved me and took good care of me. She said that children are a special blessing from one's past life. Every child that's born was destined to be born. And even if a child was born from someone else's womb, it doesn't change the fact that he or she has a rightful place in this world.

Nainai also said that a child who is meant for you can never be lost. Even if he somehow becomes separated from you after birth, you will eventually find your way back to each other. Nainai concluded that my relationship with her was a little jumbled up, because I was actually supposed to be her son. God must have woken up really confused one day and accidentally made me her grandson. She just couldn't hand me over to Hei Jian. She didn't think he was fit to be a parent—she believed that he would cause me to suffer great pain and hardships in the future. Maybe Nainai didn't love Hei Jian anymore? In the end, Nainai left her old ancestral home to her niece because her niece promised to give her a proper burial. Hei Jian had to pay rent to his cousin to keep living in that house.

"No, I don't hate her," Hei Jian said of Nainai at her graveside. "She looked after me for over twenty years. Twenty years . . . that's more than seven thousand days! And I remember each of those days vividly. Even after what she has done with the house, I don't hate her. And I never will." But he seemed to really despise Nainai's niece. He would gnash his teeth at the very sight of her, and he threw away all the bags of cookies and candy she gave me on Qing Ming—the Tomb Sweeping Festival.

Every year during the festival, Hei Jian would visit Nainai's grave at the local cemetery. He would kneel and bow before her tombstone. Then he would sit and recount stories of his childhood spent with her. Stories about how Nainai had kissed him or spanked him. Stories of their love for each other.

I pestered Hei Jian to tell me those stories again and again. I would say, "Hei Jian, I'm so jealous of you. You had Nainai as your mom. Why couldn't Nainai be my mom too?"

"Silly," Hei Jian would reply. "How can someone be both your grandma and your mom?" Then he'd say, "Don't worry, I'll find you a good mom. Promise."

But as soon as Qing Ming passed, Hei Jian would always change his mind and go back on his word. "No, I can't simply go marry someone just cause you need a mom. I can't sell myself out because of you," he'd snap. "Sure, a father has to look out for his son, but a father is also a human being who needs a life."

Of course Hei Jian could do whatever he wanted. I was never in a position to change or pressure him. Kids are powerless like that. But I didn't want to be like him when I grew up. I wanted to have a warm, quiet, comfortable home like my classmates did. I would buy groceries as soon as I got off work, then go home and cook dinner straight away. I would never beat my partner, and we'd have kids—after we got married, of course. And I would never be divorced. I planned to eat three good, wholesome meals per day. No staying out at night or staying up late. And no drinking. I would go to bed early every day and get up early the next morning. All my classmates' families were like that. That's why they all looked rosy and chubby, and could run really fast. Unlike me.

The teachers back at my old school used to say that I had character. As soon as I heard it, I knew that in their mind "having character" was the same as being a weirdo. And I really, really hated the pitiful look in their eyes whenever they told me that.

Most days, I just wanted to be a normal, happy kid.

I didn't care what grades I got or how I looked, I just needed to be ordinary, average, normal. But Hei Jian always wanted me to be anything but ordinary. He'd taught me to wear clothes with character—ones that stand out from the crowd—even before I was four years old. If I wanted to listen to kids' music or songs that everybody else listened to (like those by Jay Chou, my favorite singer), Hei Jian would say, "What the hell? Turn it off! Those songs are garbage."

Hei Jian would only buy music CDs with foreign words on their covers; he mostly listened to rock 'n' roll. So, growing up, I got to listen to plenty of rock 'n' roll. When I was in the third grade, I became obsessed with the music of No. 43 Baojia Street, a Chinese rock band. When I started to hum the tune of "Hey~ his name is Li Jianguo" in class, my teacher and classmates all turned around to look at me as if I was some alien or lunatic.

Hei Jian was really going to leave me this time. There was no way around it. After he walked me to the student dormitory and showed me my bed, he took me out for a meal. We ordered a small hotpot, and he drank a beer and tried to confide in me about something. But I wasn't paying attention to a word he was saying. I just stared at his mouth the whole time. His mouth was quite busy—he was trying to chat while chugging down beer and chewing on food at the same time. His lips were turning greasy and flaming red.

"Hey kiddo, why aren't you eating?" Hei Jian asked.

"I'm not hungry," I replied.

Hei Jian opened his mouth to say something, but paused before making any sound.

"Hey, Bai Jian," he said finally. "I know what you're thinking. Don't worry. I'm coming back to see you in one month. Maybe even less than a month, maybe in two weeks. But I will never abandon you. I swear. Think about it—there's just two of us now. How could I be so silly not to want to be with my only family in the world?

"Of course, I don't want to leave you here all by yourself," Hei Jian went on, trying to sound reassuring. "But we have to survive and find a way to live better than the average person. We'll buy a car and a house one day, and then I will send you to study abroad. But I need money to pay for all that. How can I get more money without first going out to earn it?"

I nodded. I knew money was important. Without it, we couldn't make rent. Or pay for electricity, or my school fees, or the food on our table. I felt like Hei Jian was going to ask in his next breath, *Hey Bai Jian, got any change on you?*

Usually, Hei Jian would give me some allowance money the day he got paid. And when he ran out, he would ask me for some of it back. By the time he came to me to ask for change that usually meant he hadn't got a cent left on him, which also meant that we were going to need to tighten our belts for a while.

There was a particularly tough period when we could only afford to eat boiled rice once a day, for an entire week. By the end of that week, I was so starved and weak, I could hardly walk. Fortunately, we got a chance to visit the countryside several days later. When night fell, we snuck into a farmer's field and stole a bunch of corn. Then we heated a big pot of water over a campfire and boiled the corn. It smelled and tasted like heaven.

"Come on, give me a hug!" Hei Jian pulled me close after finishing the hotpot meal. He squeezed his arms around me so tightly, I thought I was getting crushed. Then he rushed off like the wind, his long hair fluttering in the fall breeze like a thousand tiny hands waving me goodbye. Just before he got into a taxicab, Hei Jian did look back and wave at me. I was crying. Obviously, he couldn't hear me. There was too much noise around us. So, I just kept crying and crying and crying, out loud.

The taxi rolled away. I was truly alone in the city.

When I returned to the student dorm, my roommates—who had been playing some game together—turned around to examine me. I stood out among them. I was pale and skinny. My arms dangled about me like thin hockey sticks, while their arms were chunky and muscular, arms that looked almost as thick as my fists.

I envied them.

## ☁ Chapter 3

It was a Wet and Gloomy Day

The first Friday I spent at my new school was a wet and gloomy day. I think I might have developed the ability to summon rain with my mind, because, when I had gotten up early that morning, the sky was still sunny and cloudless. As I stood on the front steps of the main school building, peering up, I thought, Oh God, please make it rain! Make it rain so hard that the sky and earth will become one big, wet, blurry mess. So that no one inside will want to leave, and no one outside can get in. And I can just stand under that covered corridor in the school yard and watch the rain fall down all evening and not have to go anywhere . . . in short, I made a secret, selfish wish that my classmates wouldn't be able to go home for the weekend, and that we would all be stuck at school together.

Shortly after I made that wish, it started to rain. It poured hard during the first period, and I was overjoyed. I pored over my textbooks with more enthusiasm than ever before. But halfway through the afternoon, the rain stopped.

Some parents were already waiting eagerly outside our classroom. I glanced toward them—a sea of unfamiliar faces—and instantly made up my mind to never look that way again. It had been barely one week since I arrived here, and Hei Jian's next visit wasn't until the following month. How was that possible?

But after a while, I couldn't help peeking at the door again. Somewhere in that crowd, I saw a whisper of blue, like a small piece of clear blue sky. That's how I knew Jing was there. She always wore blue. She adored the color, almost to the point of obsession. Her clothes, watches, accessories, and socks were all blue. Even her toothbrush and bath towels were blue.

I don't like blue. I think it's kind of boring. I like black the best. I also like yellow and green, the official colors of the Brazilian soccer team. Jing once said, "Bai Jian, based on your color preferences, you will surely become a very powerful and respectable man." I was delighted to hear her say that, because everybody else only commented on how skinny and malnourished I looked. They said I seemed "wimpy and frail, like a girl."

"The color black usually symbolizes grief and mourning," Jing said. "So, Bai Jian, why are you feeling unhappy? Do you always feel sad?"

"No," I said. "I'm not sad or upset about anything. Most of the time, I just don't think there's much out there to be happy about."

Ever since we first met, Jing has been trying to figure me out. She said that she wanted to be my friend. Once or twice, she came super close to uncovering my innermost thoughts. So close. But in the end, she just gently poked her head in and then quickly retreated. This was back when the three of us were still living together under one roof.

One day, Jing had just finished washing my hair and was starting to blow-dry it. Amid the whirring noise of the hair dryer, she examined the back of my head and said, "Bai Jian, your head is shaped like a Northerner's. How come a person growing up in the South has the flat head of a Northerner?"

"My head got squashed because I slept on it too much as a baby," I said.

"Why were you sleeping so much?"

"Probably because I had a lot to think about. I spent most of my days lying in bed, staring at the ceiling and pondering all kind of questions."

Jing laughed aloud. "Care to share what kind of questions were on your mind?"

"Oh, like why do the other babies drink milk from their mothers' breasts, while I had to drink cow's milk from a bottle?"

Jing had chortled so hard, she nearly fell out of her chair. She couldn't hold the hair dryer steady in her hand any longer.

Watching tears roll down Jing's face, I asked, "Was that funny?"

Jing stopped laughing and looked at me silently. Then she drew close and pressed my head against her chest, whispering. "Bai Jian, let's not dwell on the past anymore. We should look toward the future and think about happy things."

"I'm not exactly unhappy," I replied. "I just tend to think about a bunch of random stuff. And sometimes, I don't even know what I'm thinking about."

"Do you dream when you fall asleep? Can you tell me about your dreams?" Jing asked.

So I told her about the dream I'd had the night before. "There was this little white mouse that was scurrying around, searching for something. It kept looking and looking, but couldn't find whatever that thing was. In the end, it was crushed by a giant foot that came down from the sky."

After that, things turned extra quiet. Jing didn't reply for a long time. Finally, she said, "Bai Jian, are you scared of sleeping by yourself?"

"Yes," I admitted.

"Alright then," she said. "Tonight, you are welcome to sleep with us."

Just then, the phone rang. Jing went to pick it up. She mumbled a few words and closed the bedroom door behind her. After hanging up the phone, Jing rushed out the door. It was 9 p.m. sharp.

I climbed into bed alone. When I woke up again, it was already past midnight. The noise coming from the TV must have woken me up. Hei Jian was watching a soccer game. I overheard Jing say to him, "I promised Bai Jian that he could sleep with us tonight."

And Hei Jian replied, "Oh, that's a terrible idea, don't you think?"

"But he's still just a kid . . ."

I was disappointed Jing didn't fight harder for me. I thought to myself, Why can't you try to push back a bit more? Or hold your ground for just a little longer?! I went back to sleep, feeling angry and disappointed. Later on, I would come to realize that many other kids have experienced similar moments of frustration—that they have also been angry and disappointed at grown-ups. It's so unfair that adults, who aren't even afraid of the dark, can sleep in the company of other adults, while we kids have to sleep by ourselves.

It was extra hard to get out of the classroom with all the students crowded around the door like dumplings in a pot. Jing saw me as I stood back alone in the middle of the classroom. She smiled and waved at me. I nodded.

Jing has a petite frame. Like I expected, she was decked out in light blue from head to toe. I noticed something else just now: even her veins were light blue. No wonder she was so fond of that color. Then I looked down instinctively at the veins on my arm. Phew, they weren't black.

Jing's tiny rental apartment doesn't have a kitchen so we couldn't cook. We had to go out to eat. Jing always skipped dinner—she wanted to stay in shape. As she watched me eat, she asked me how the food was at my school cafeteria. "Delicious," I said. "And not spicy at all."

Whenever I ate with Hei Jian, my butthole would burn and tingle and my belly would bloat up like a bag of firecrackers, ready to explode at any moment. That's because Hei Jian likes to make everything extra spicy. Often, after eating the stuff he made, even my tears would taste spicy. Jing was much better at selecting food than Hei Jian. She would first ask me what I wanted to eat, then she would always make sure there was something on the table that appealed to me. The

Jing living in this one-bedroom apartment felt a bit different than the Jing who had lived with me and Hei Jian though. Probably because her new place was so small and cramped.

I took extra care not to touch anything fragile around here, like the vase on the table, or the small stool near my feet, or the bottles of wine strewn about the place.

"Do you like to drink wine?" I asked.

Jing always kept a wine glass near the foot of the bed. That's why I didn't want to get too close to her bed. I was afraid of accidentally knocking it over. She said that she liked to have a glass of wine before going to bed because, after drinking the wine, she would fall asleep easier and have more pleasant dreams.

"Why do you have trouble sleeping?" I asked.

"When you grow to be as old as me, you will understand. Every adult has some kind of sleep issue."

But Hei Jian didn't seem to have any trouble with sleep, I thought to myself. He always slept soundly through the night, even after a big fight with Jing. As soon as his head touched the pillow, he would pass out and start to snore loudly. Then he would wake up the next morning and apologize to Jing.

"Hey Bai Jian, has Hei Jian called you yet?" Jing asked.

"Yes."

"Did anyone else come to visit you at school?"

"Nope."

"I bet your dorm's phone line gets quite clogged up at night, what with all the parents trying to talk with their kids."

"Actually, no. We all get together to play after finishing our homework. Nobody wants to talk with their parents—the grown-ups just ask the same things over and over. 'What did you eat today?' or 'Did you remember to change your outfit?' They throw so many silly questions at us and just treat us like we're still a bunch of kindergarteners."

"Is that so? Then what questions do you think parents should ask?"

"I don't know. They seem to only pay attention to the small details . . . superficial stuff. Like, as long as we're properly dressed and not starving or sick, then all's well. In fact, the things they care about the most are the stuff *we* care about the least. Maybe they believe that by nagging at us every day, they're showing us love and affection. But are we truly happy? Do they actually care to know?"

"So, Bai Jian, let me ask you: Are you happy?"

"Why ask me? I'm talking about the other kids, not me."

"But I really want to know. Seriously, I want to hear your answer."

"Are *you* happy?" I fired it back at her.

"Well, that question is too big for me to answer right now." Jing froze up for a moment before adding, "Bai Jian, you scare me sometimes. Why do I always feel like a fool in front of you? Can't you be just a little less sharp?"

I sensed that Jing was getting a little upset, so I had to change the subject. I shouldn't have tripped her up like that—sometimes grown-ups can be more childish and temperamental than us kids. So, I said, "Jing, let's play a game. It's called Fortune-Telling."

"What? You know how to tell fortunes?"

"Um, no. That's just the name of a popular game we play at school. All you have to do is answer ten questions. For each question, you can give me up to three answers. For example, what's your favorite color?"

"Blue, blue, and blue," Jing answered without hesitating.

"What's your favorite mode of transportation?"

"By airplane," she replied.

"Which guy do you love the most?"

"You mean, someone from real life?" Jing asked with all seriousness.

"Yes. It has to be a real, living person."

"Hei Jian, Brad Pitt, and Angus Tung."

After going through the entire list of questions, I tallied up her answers and did a quick analysis to figure out Jing's fortune. "You'll be dressed in a light blue wedding gown and travel to heaven in an airplane to marry Hei Jian. Then, you will become lovers with Angus Tung and never have any kids of your own."

Jing laughed, and then, almost in an instant, started crying. Stunned, I didn't know how to respond. With tears still streaming down her cheeks, Jing got up and headed toward the bathroom. Grown-ups often run to the bathroom when they come across a complicated problem. It's like their safe space.

A few minutes later, Jing reemerged. Putting on her usual smile, she announced, "Well, that stuff was all nonsense. I forgot it was just a game. How stupid of me to have taken it so seriously!" She proceeded to check over my homework and fill out the weekly parental feedback section. Then she helped me to get ready for bed.

"Bai Jian, do you think adults and children can become good friends?" she asked.

"Of course they can!" I replied.

"But the two of us may no longer be friends, since Hei Jian and I have split up. He will find you a new mom eventually. You will soon have a new life and forget about me." She looked distraught.

"Back when we used to live under the same roof, we were all happy and content, right?"

I let out a long and heavy sigh.

"What's wrong?" Jing asked.

I let the words spill out from my heart. "I just want to live by myself, in a home of my own. I don't want to drift around with Hei Jian anymore. Every time he falls in love, I have to follow him and meet a new auntie. At first, everybody gets along fine, and the new auntie is really nice to me. But soon, things start to go downhill: the arguments, the fighting, another break-up . . . and then, they stop caring about each other. The auntie suddenly acts like she hates me. That really bothers me. Sometimes, I get the feeling that grown-ups are much more selfish and unreasonable than children. Because even when they're fully capable of controlling their actions and emotions, they still choose to behave like the sky is falling and the world is ending. I don't want to be like that when I grow up."

Jing didn't say anything. But after I finished, when I was about to fall asleep on the floor, she got up and gave me a big hug and carried me into her bed. She told me to sleep on my side so that we could snuggle up, facing the same direction. Then she whispered into my ear, "Bai Jian, you don't have to sleep on the floor anymore. From now on, we can share the same bed. We were once as close as mother and son. Let's keep it that way, okay?"

At first, I wasn't used to sleeping in that position. But soon I felt cozy and warm again. Jing's body had a sweet, powdery fragrance, like the scent of jasmine flowers or orchids. Her fingers glided over my hair and gently grazed my neck. And she said, "Bai Jian, you're too thin. You should eat more."

I said I didn't have a big appetite. I was never that interested in food.

Jing suddenly thought of a new question for me. "Do you remember anyone else putting you to bed like this?"

"Yes, my nainai."

"Who else?"

"Hei Jian. Sometimes."

"And who else?"

"Nobody else. Except you."

If I was being completely honest, there was one other person who had let me fall asleep in her arms. It was one of Hei Jian's girlfriends, before Jing. That auntie had been just as smitten with Hei Jian as Jing once was. And that relationship had, unsurprisingly, also ended after a big fight.

Jing wrapped her arms around me and said, "Bai Jian, it would be so wonderful if you were my son. You're so smart and handsome. I would spoil you and offer you all the love in the world."

I felt a stinging sensation in my eyes. Yes, how wonderful that would be. I would no longer be a weirdo, or an outsider. No one would look at me with that pitiful gaze again. I would be able to pronounce the word loud and clear: "Mom."

I almost never said it while alone. The one time I attempted to say that word aloud, I choked up and made a strange, garbled noise—not at all like my classmates, who rattled off various funny and intimate versions, letting the syllable roll off their tongue so naturally and smoothly. Ever since then, I'd refused even to try to say it.

Whenever Hei Jian and that old ex-girlfriend of his argued, she would point her finger angrily at me, shouting at Hei Jian at the top of her lungs, "Did you really think I could love this child of yours? I hate him! Hate him! From the very beginning, I was just doing it to please you. I've disliked him from the moment I laid eyes on him. Why can't you and I have our own child? I dare you to have one with me! . . . Oh? You can't? I bet the idea hadn't even crossed your mind. You've never loved me. This whole time, Hei Jian, you were just stringing me along!"

I remember now—her name was Yan. She owned a clothing shop. She dressed well and ate well and spent lavishly on expensive things. For Chinese New Year, she gave me a red envelope stuffed with two hundred yuan. But of course, Hei Jian took the money as soon as she left. Hei Jian always managed to dig out all the red-envelope money from my pockets. Nothing I could do about it.

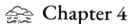 **Chapter 4**

It was Grey and Overcast on Fall Family Sports Day

The sky was grey and overcast on the school's annual Fall Family Sports Day. Our head teacher had sent an invitation letter to all parents several days ahead, asking them to join our class for a day of fun games and friendly competition.

Who should I give this letter to? Hei Jian wouldn't be able to make it as the event would take place way before his next monthly visit. And I had no way of contacting him anyway—I didn't know his new cell number. Not that I have a crappy memory or anything. His numbers kept changing because he either lost his phone or switched jobs. My theory is that since Hei Jian likes to jump around so much, he must have been a Chinese checkers player in his previous life.

Did Jing count as my parent? I imagined Jing joining me on Fall Family Sports Day. But I wasn't sure if she would want to. After her breakup with Hei Jian, she looked even more sad and withdrawn. Her precious blue dresses kept her away from the crowd, just like the man named Hei Jian kept her away from other suitors. Ultimately, I still decided to give Jing the letter, hoping that the atmosphere of the event would lift her spirits a little even if she wasn't a fan of big crowds.

I didn't expect her to be so excited to receive my invite. "Really? Can I *really* join you for your school's family event? This will be a new experience for me. I hope I won't embarrass you!" she babbled. "And your classmates' moms, are they all beautiful and elegant?"

"Nah, I think you are the prettiest m—of them all." I stopped short of saying the word in the middle of the sentence. Technically, since Hei Jian and Jing had officially broken up, I no longer had any direct connection to her. We were just tapping into the goodwill banked up from our past interactions. Maybe that account was already running out of funds, and we were going into overdraft mode.

When Fall Family Sports Day arrived, Jing was in quite a different mood. For most of the morning, she sat alone in the far corner of the school yard, staring blankly into space. Occasionally, she would come over and participate in an event. But she just couldn't relax enough to immerse herself in any of the games. She seemed uncomfortably tense—her body was stiff and clumsy.

Many other parents came; some grandparents also showed up. For games like shooting hoops, balloon popping, and jumping rope, there was strength in numbers. They totally destroyed us. Even during the less sporty games, Jing and I kept losing points for no good reason. As a team, we must have seemed so weak and pathetic on the field. Unlike the larger families, there was no one else to cheer for us. Whenever another team fell behind, there was usually a squad of people gathered around them: giggling, shouting, waving, rooting them on. I think that's what family is all about. It's like what Nainai had told me before— people who are related by blood share a special, unbreakable bond.

Eventually it was our turn to do the three-legged race. With one of our legs tied together, Jing and I tripped and stumbled at every turn, falling to the ground again and again in the most awkward poses. Waves of laughter rose up around us. When we were done, Jing and I rushed to free our legs, then immediately shot up and tossed the rope ties away like they were pieces of burning coal. I think in that moment we both resented each other a little, but neither of us wanted to admit it publicly. One thing was for sure: we had both completely lost interest in the games. I ripped the number tag off my jersey and plopped myself down near the edge of the ball court. Jing also sat down. We made sure to put a good distance between us and for the next while refused to make eye contact with each other.

Eventually, the last event of the morning wrapped up. Jing stayed quiet and motionless in the far corner of the track field, watching everyone else, walled off by her pale blue bubble. I could tell that she was envious of the other smiling parents. Her face was overcast. Maybe embarrassment, and self doubt? Sadly, that wasn't something I could help her with.

I once heard Jing say to Hei Jian, "You know, I'm already thirty-one. I can't continue to live my life like this . . . hanging around you . . . no direction, no plan. I want to get married, Hei Jian. I want to have kids. Will you help me with those things? If the answer is no, then we should go our separate ways."

But they didn't split up after she said that, or they separated for a day and then quickly made up, because the next time Hei Jian and I went to see Jing, they looked perfectly happy together—as if that previous day's conversation had never taken place. Later on, Hei Jian teased Jing, "Didn't you say you want to get married and have kids? Where's your husband? Where are your kids?"

"Oh, they're all sitting at home, waiting for my return," Jing retorted.

Hei Jian smacked her shoulder gently. "Nobody can touch my woman. Just let them try."

But soon after that, I discovered the truth. I woke up from my nap one day and was about to open my eyes when I heard Jing say quietly, "A matchmaker just sent me some info on this guy. He seems like a nice person. I want to go meet him."

A few moments later, Hei Jian replied in a drowsy voice, "Sure. You're a good woman. You deserve a nice life. I sincerely hope your date with him goes well." Then, after an even longer pause, he sighed. "I've always had the worst luck with women. All the good ones leave me in the end."

"Why didn't you try to keep some of those good women around?"

"I couldn't—I didn't plant the right trees."

"Why not start planting now? What are you waiting for?"

"Hey, stop lecturing me. You're already flown away from me. And you know how I am—I have a different way of thinking than most. Instead of planting my own trees and all that, I like to find ones already grown."

"So *that's* how it is. If you had told me this earlier, I wouldn't have stuck around for so long and wasted your precious time!" Jing's voice was simmering with anger, so I rolled noisily in my bed then and made a big yawn, to show them that I was waking up.

Before Fall Family Sports Day was over, Jing came up to me and said, "Hey Bai Jian, I'm afraid I have to skip out now. I took the morning off and must get back to work." She rushed away before I could respond.

The final event of the day was the awards ceremony. All the families who had won a medal lifted their kids high in the air and started to snap photos. I was about to turn and walk away when my teacher called to me, "Don't go yet, Bai Jian. There's an award for you too. Even though you and your mom didn't rank high enough to win any sporting medal, you still get an award for participating!"

My face began to flush and burn. Hearing my teacher call Jing my "mom" made me feel all weird and cringey. Plus, getting only a consolation prize was super embarrassing. Some of my classmates who overheard the teacher's comments burst out laughing. One person hollered, "Nice prize . . . for scoring a big, fat zero!"

I vowed to never participate in any silly family games days again. I'd rather go attend a real track and field competition, where I could long jump, high jump, sprint, and hurdle on my own. And I would score higher than anybody else—that is, as long as I wasn't paired up with other people. I trust in my own strength. And when the time was right, I was going to unleash my full power, letting it erupt from my fiery core like a volcano. I would take the world by storm!

Probably because of all that running, jumping, and sweating during Fall Family Sports Day, I caught a cold. My body burned with a high fever all evening. I felt like a piece of red yam being roasted over a campfire. The dorm parent was terrified—she kept asking me for Hei Jian's phone number. I hemmed and hawed and came up with a different number each time. Of course, she couldn't do anything with them. I gulped down a whole bunch of cold medicine, but my fever refused to come down. Eventually, for whatever reason, Jing's phone number popped into my head.

Jing clutched my hand the whole time we sat in the hospital's waiting room, and she stayed by my side during all the injections and infusions. I thought about Hei Jian only briefly as the night got late, then I drifted off to sleep. I can't remember what my dream was about. Only that I woke up screaming for my mom and that Jing hugged me and started crying herself. She asked, "Bai Jian, do you really wish your mom was here with you?"

"No," I said. "Don't take it too seriously. I was just dreaming. Everybody dreams."

"I hate it when you put on this tough-looking armor and pretend to be invincible," Jing said. "Can't you just relax a little, and let yourself be a kid?"

"What's so great about being a kid? Nobody really cares about kids—they are either your pet or your burden. Why bring kids into this world if you're just going to ignore or hurt them?"

Jing had tears on her face. "Bai Jian, can I help you get your mom back? As long as she's alive, I promise I will find her, one way or another."

"No. If she truly wanted me, she would have come for me long ago."

"But a child shouldn't be kept away from his mom. Without a mother's love, he's going to see the world as a much colder and darker place. He may grow up full of sadness and bitterness. He may have difficulty giving and accepting love later on in life."

"Don't be so certain about that," I said. "Am I a cold, bitter, uncaring person? Many people enjoy eating frogs and snakes, but I've never eaten them. I can't bring myself to do it, because even ugly, poisonous vermin have emotions and feelings. Aren't humans who kill and eat exotic animals the cold-hearted ones? And the funny thing is, most of those people grew up with loving moms!"

"I can't talk you out of it, but I know you are a bit off in your thinking. It's not too late though—you just need a mother to guide you back on track."

Jing stayed home from work the following day. She took me to see another doctor. When we went back to her apartment, she made me porridge, then she spent the rest of the day reading books to me and chatting with me. I felt like a real patient, and I really enjoyed being treated like one.

"Do you miss Hei Jian?" Jing asked. "Wanna give him a call?"

"No!" I shook my head decisively. I felt anxious and tense even thinking about Hei Jian. He was like a ticking bomb without a set timer, ready to explode anytime and screw everything up. For now, all I wanted was a little peace and calm. Nothing exciting, just soft, soothing sounds; warm, gentle air; mild-tasting foods.

Three days later, I went back to school, and my life returned to the way it was before I got sick. Between classes, I would think about the time I spent at Jing's place. I didn't know which lifestyle I preferred more—the loud, chaotic life with Hei Jian that brimmed with excitement and surprise, or the quiet, relaxed life with Jing where things had a predictable rhythm and schedule; where each hour of the day was pre-programmed with its specific activity. One thing was clear: if I ever had to live with both of them at the same time again, the situation would become much more complicated. It wouldn't just be getting peace half of the time and chaos the other half. I'm not sure how to explain it . . . but I knew that I would just end up feeling lonely and left out. It's like the two of them belonged in a world of their own when they were together. Even if they were constantly arguing, fighting, and cursing each other to death, I was still the outsider. And if I tried to draw closer to one of them, I worried that I was making the other person feel alone and left out too.

After I recovered from my bout of illness, I felt miserable for a long time. It was the feeling of being pushed out of other peoples' lives—of being abandoned and forgotten. I was suddenly thrown from the soft, cushy clouds of love and attention to the cold, hard ground below. How I wished to be sick again! When you're sick, people come over and surround you with kindness and warmth. They take care of you and lift you up into clouds.

❄ **Chapter 5**

The First Snowfall Landed on a Wednesday

The first snowfall of the season landed on a Wednesday. The snowflakes were massive—as big as rice balls. It was frigid inside our classroom, but we were so excited to go out and play, we didn't mind the cold at all. After dinner, we needed no reminder from our teachers to start tackling our homework, because once we finished, we planned to go out to the schoolyard and build a snowman. I was neck deep in work when the teacher on evening duty asked me to step out of class and go meet someone.

She was a pretty-looking stranger. As soon as she saw me, she smiled. It was so weird. I was sure I had never seen her before, but somehow, her smile seemed kind of . . . familiar. I started to panic inside.

"Is your name Bai Jian?" she asked as she approached me slowly.

I nodded and stepped back. Bummer! There was a wall behind me.

"I'm Mom. Your mother."

I guess I could have laughed, gasped, or made some other silly or dramatic facial expression. But instead, I managed to squeeze out exactly one word.

"Oh!"

She stroked my head. "Goodness, you are all grown up!"

I had nowhere to escape. So I asked, "How did you know I was here?"

"Jing told me," she replied. She kept looking at me like I was some kind of bizarre, exotic specimen on display at a museum. I lowered my head and stared at the floor.

"Wow, I didn't expect you to be so tall already! And us living so close. . . . You know, I recognized you the moment I saw you! I always thought that I would never see you again in my lifetime." She touched my hand, then pinched my arm. "You're too skinny. Have you been eating alright?"

I said, "Yes, I eat very well. I just can't seem to put on any weight."

We sat down, and for a long time, she was quiet. She didn't ask me about Hei Jian at all. She just kept her eyes on me, scanning up and down, studying me from head to toe. She smelled like strong perfume and her hair was permed into dense curls. She wore makeup and sported a bunch of shiny rings on her fingers. She looked like one of those chic girls on the streets. I sensed a world of difference between her and Hei Jian. Over the years, I'd also become quite familiar with Hei Jian's taste in women. All his ex-girlfriends had long, straight hair, wore simple clothes, and did not put on heavy makeup or glitzy jewelry.

If you were to put the three of us side by side—Hei Jian, me, and this lady—and snap a photo, I don't think it would end up looking like a family portrait.

"Do you hate me?" she asked.

I shook my head. It was true. I didn't hate her, because I rarely thought about her. But I can't say that I liked her either. She felt like any other auntie to me—no more and no less.

She wanted to take me to McDonald's. I said I couldn't go because our school had a pretty strict policy against students eating off campus on weekdays. (That wasn't exactly true. But I was tired of that kind of superficial display of affection. Grown-ups liked to bribe kids with food, like Happy Meals. As if that's the only thing they can imagine us wanting, and all that they can offer.)

She also said she'd take me clothes shopping, which is another activity that didn't interest me. Besides buying us food or clothes, did the grown-ups have other ideas for what to do with children? I was getting really annoyed by their antics. In the past, whenever I met Hei Jian's newest girlfriend—or, if his girlfriend at the time was in a good mood—they would buy me lots of snacks and new clothes. I was the soccer field of Hei Jian's love life, one which his girlfriends watered generously and fertilized diligently, until one day they mowed it all down.

Sometimes those expensive gifts came too readily and unexpectedly. Once, an auntie bought me a suit from Rainbow Childhood, to please Hei Jian of course. That jacket alone cost over three hundred yuan. When Hei Jian saw it, he said, "Damn, it's more expensive than any of my outfits!" But Hei Jian wasn't so fond of that lady, so after gifting me just one set of clothes, she vanished from our lives. Most of my classmates at my old school were jealous of me because I would randomly receive these nice, expensive things. But they had no idea how dismal my life turned when the girlfriends left.

The lady who introduced herself as my mom returned the next day to school. She wrote her name inside my palm. That was the first time I learned it: Jie.

She said she wanted to spend the upcoming Lunar New Year with me. I told her that Hei Jian was coming back to town soon. But she insisted that I join her for New Year's Eve. She said that from now on, we should try to stay together. I said I needed to ask Hei Jian first. Maybe my reply upset her. She was emphatic that she had never not wanted me. She said that she left me because Hei Jian was being so cold and cruel to her. At the time, she had just wanted to punish him, to give him a taste his own bitter medicine. And in spite of it all, she still loved me.

I guess a mother who is so determined to punish a man she loved she could stand to be separated from her own child for eleven years is . . . probably not your average mom. In my opinion, she was no better than Hei Jian at being a parent.

She asked me if I missed her. And as she spoke, she brought her makeup-glazed face close to mine. So close, I could see each of her thick, curled eyelashes and the lumpy coat of charcoal-black mascara caked onto them. Fine wrinkles creased the skin under her eyes. A dab of bright red blush marked her cheekbones. She tried to give me a kiss. Her lips were plump, glossy, and blood red. They did not look natural.

I didn't know how to respond to her question. I mean, I had thought about her from time to time. Each time, I would try to paint a picture of her in my head. She had no concrete physical features—she was more of an abstract concept, a symbol of the word "Mom." Yet when that imaginary figure actually came to life, I realized I felt more estranged from her than ever before.

Glancing at her from a distance, I could see her broad forehead, slim chin, and prominent features that, when turned to the side, revealed a well-defined profile. But once she moved too close to me, I could only see the parts and portions of her face that had been painted over. And I didn't like what I saw.

Jie took me to her home, a narrow and crowded space. There were many others who also lived there. They peered at me curiously and furtively through the corners of their eyes, like stealthy thieves. When I looked in their direction, they quickly averted their gaze. Later I overheard them talking in the kitchen.

"Jie, you can't just bring him over on a whim. Have you talked with his dad?"

"What's there to talk about? We haven't spoken in years."

"But you can't just leave things like this. You should either marry him or forget about the whole thing."

"Marriage is definitely out of the question. He's got his own life now," Jie replied.

"Are you planning to raise the boy all by yourself? Don't be deceived by his innocent looks—it's no lark raising a child when you can barely support yourself."

"But hasn't his dad been raising him by himself?"

"It's different for a man. A man can always find another woman to help him take care of his child. It's much harder for a woman to find a man willing to do the same."

"Well, I'm perfectly capable of looking after him on my own," Jie insisted.

"No, hon, we can't have you do that! You've already brought us plenty of trouble and headaches. Let us live in peace, will ya?"

"But what am I supposed to do now?"

"Like I said before, you either get married, or walk away," one person said. "You walked out of the kid's life when he was a lot younger. What's stopping you from doing it now?"

"Yeah, if you keep him around, you'll be doing the boy's dad a huge favor," someone else chimed in. "He was probably trying to get out of his fatherly duties, or he wouldn't have sent his son to a boarding school. If you take over now, do you think the boy will grow up thanking you and remembering your kindness? Let me tell you, if you haven't changed his dirty diapers from day one, you just won't have that kind of special bond with him. It's not like you can make up for that sort of thing. So, why bother?"

It was a really rough and chaotic week for me. After I returned from Jie's place, Jing came to visit me at school.

"Did your mom come to find you?" she asked.

I nodded.

"Did things go well?"

I nodded again. I was at a loss for words. I didn't know how to describe the way I felt, so I resorted to nodding. Nodding didn't mean I agreed with what was being said.

"How wonderful! You've finally met your mother. Now my job is done. I should leave." But as soon as Jing finished speaking, she burst into tears. "Bai Jian, you won't forget about me or the good times we had together . . . right?"

I nodded again.

"Am I still picking you up on Fridays?"

I looked at her, not wanting to nod anymore. I didn't know what fate had in store for me this coming Friday.

"Will your mom be picking you up then?"

"She hasn't mentioned it."

Jing left. I could tell she was having a difficult time. She sobbed as she walked away. "You have to remember me, okay? I will miss you, Bai Jian."

Before she got more than a few steps out, Jing came running back. "Actually . . . it's best if you forget me," she continued. "Stay with your mom and enjoy your life together. It's good for a child to be with his mother."

After she was gone, I stood there with my feet rooted to the ground, not knowing what I was thinking or even what to think.

I dreaded the next Friday, because all of a sudden, I didn't have any idea where I was supposed to go. Luckily, Hei Jian called. I told him what Jie had said. I wanted him to help me decide where to go. But I didn't expect him to get so upset when he heard that Jie invited me to spend New Year's Eve with her.

"Who does she think she is, trying to cozy up to you after neglecting you for so long," he fumed. "DON'T go!"

I fired back: "But I don't want to eat greasy fast food or instant noodles on New Year's Eve, or stay up all night watching movies with you! You know what I saw at her place? A kitchen lined with pots, pans, and cooking utensils. An entire wall of spices—rows and rows of them! I've never seen such a well-stocked kitchen before. I don't need to talk to her about feelings and stuff, I just want to have a good New Year's Eve. Is that not allowed?"

Hei Jian fell silent. I think I may not have chosen the best words to express myself. I was rambling, and I probably sounded very materialistic. But I didn't feel like apologizing. We were both silent for a while on the phone. Then Hei Jian spoke up:

"Listen kiddo, I've always given you plenty of freedom to do what you want. But this is a special situation. In this case, you've got to listen to me. Try to stand in my shoes. For years, I've worked so hard to raise you. I even gave up my college education for you and abandoned my dreams. I could have put you up for adoption, but I chose not to. Because I loved you and treasured you too much. But the moment that woman appeared, you shifted your loyalties to her, no questions asked. Think about it. How would you feel if you studied hard for your finals and scored well, only to discover that you took the exam for somebody else?"

In the end, I promised Hei Jian that I wouldn't go spend New Year's Eve with Jie, and that I would wait for him to come back to town and pick me up for the holiday. I also told Hei Jian that it was Jing who located my mom and asked her to visit me.

"I knew it," Hei Jian grunted. "She doesn't want to help me take care of you anymore, so she found a nice way to get out of it."

I said that was not Jing's real intent. She just wanted to—

"Oh hell," he interrupted me. "You know fuck all!"

On Friday afternoon, Jie came over. She took me to a place where several women were seated around a square table, chitchatting and playing mahjong. They took turns coming up to me and talking with me for a bit before returning to the game. Jie joined them at the table too.

I found a small vanity in the corner of the room, where I sat down and began to do my homework. The strong, cloying scent of powders and perfume prickled my nose and made me sneeze.

Once during the mahjong night, Jia came over to check on me. She said she wanted to read the essay I was writing. There were several essays in my notebook, each on a different topic. Whenever my teacher asked us to write an essay about people, I wrote about Hei Jian, because there was no one else to write about.

Jie asked me, "Have you ever tried to write an essay about your mom?"

I told her that our teachers wanted us to write things that are true and honest.

"I mustn't leave you anymore. You may really end up disowning me!" Jie was about to say something else, but she was called away by her friends at the table.

They started to lecture her again. "Don't be so paranoid. Your son is your son, and always will be. Nobody can take him from you. Even if you were to leave him, he would still come running back to you! Haven't you heard the saying 'blood is thicker than water'? Family cannot get away from family. On the flip side, you can't stop a child who's wild at heart from running off."

"I will never leave him again," Jie said simply.

"Oh, don't be silly. How are you going to raise him? You can't even take care of yourself. Just let the man do the hard stuff. Even if he's not the best at raising kids, at least he won't mistreat his own son. Just think about it—years down the line, you'll have a son who's all mature and grown up. You'll be able to reap the benefits without having done any backbreaking work."

After finishing my homework, I went straight to bed. The clattering of mahjong blocks being shuffled and tossed on the table woke me up several times throughout the night. Suddenly, I began to miss Jing so much. Her place was peaceful and tidy. Even when the three of us were living together, Jing was always considerate of me. If I was sleeping, she would walk around on tiptoes, quiet as a cat. She would turn on the TV gently and lower the volume. Jing was such a kind, attentive person. And she knew how to respect kids.

Wait, I just remembered something! The last time I saw her, Jing had told me that an uncle had proposed to her. She wanted to introduce him to me and get my opinion on things. She said that kids have the sharpest eyes and the keenest intuition. They can usually tell with one glance, even at a distance, whether someone is a good person. I had been glad to hear her say that, so I'd agreed to take a look for her.

When I woke up in the morning, all the mahjong players from the previous night had dispersed. I was surprised to see a dude I've never met before brushing his teeth in the bathroom. When he saw me, he nodded at me with the toothbrush still stuck in his mouth. Jie walked over to us and said, "Bai Jian, say hi to Uncle Li."

Remember what I said before? All grown-ups are alike. They can't seem to manage on their own. They're too scared to live alone—they're way more needy than us kids. It's like the end of the world or something if they can't have an adult companion. Us kids, we mostly play by ourselves and face our troubles alone.

For the most part, I'm used to meeting strangers. Strangers tended to be really nice to me at first—bribing me, trying to get me to like them and side with them. Because of that, I didn't need to worry about how to approach them or interact with them. I just needed to accept their so-called good will.

Sure enough, this Uncle Li asked me, "Where do you want to go for breakfast?"

"Wherever you like," I said. "I have no preference."

He took us to a revolving restaurant on the top floor of an upscale hotel. It had quite the extensive dim sum breakfast menu. But I wasn't all that hungry. I thought about how funny and unpredictable life was: one day, living on scallion pancakes and instant noodles with Hei Jian; another, eating inside a fancy restaurant. As we sat down on the fourteenth floor of the hotel, enjoying a breathtaking bird's-eye view of the city, I nodded or shook my head absent-mindedly at Jia and Uncle Li's endless stream of questions. And I asked myself, why *can't* I have both? Why not take Hei Jian's crispy pancakes and Jie's expensive dim sum, mix them together, then divvy up the food throughout my day? I promise not to get bored of eating the same things over and over. Just like my classmates who ate the same breakfast every morning—a cup of warm milk, a hard-boiled egg, a steamed bun.

"Hey Bai Jian, why aren't you saying much?" Jie asked. "Why just shake your head or nod? It's not very polite."

"Maybe he's at that rebellious stage, you know," Uncle Li said. "He seems rather mature for his age. Precocious."

I hate it when people called me "precocious." They think I've matured quickly because of my unique circumstances. Because of that, I often have had to go out of my way to prove otherwise. I decided to joke around to show them that I was still a child. A bubbly, playful little boy.

I turned to Jie and Uncle with a serious, straight face. "Have you heard of that story where Grown-up Pig nods his head and the Baby Pigs shake their heads?" They shook their heads together. I stared at them for a moment, then burst into a fake laughter. A second later, Uncle Li caught on and began to laugh hysterically, slapping his thigh and rocking back and forth until his chair creaked.

Jie looked flabbergasted. Uncle Li poked her side and chortled, "Your son just tricked us. He was telling us that we are Baby Pigs, and that he is a Grown-up Pig. Get it?"

Jie cracked up too. I didn't find two laughing adults all that interesting, so I turned my gaze toward the other end of the room. There were other families having breakfast with young children. Some of those kids were glancing over at us. There was an old granny with a head full of white hair. She wore gold-rimmed spectacles and a flowing red dress adorned with golden embroidery. She was playing with her grandson and chatting with him in English. I stared at them for a long while and thought of my own nainai.

Nainai didn't have that much white hair. She didn't wear expensive clothes or glasses, and she knew very little English. But she was the most gorgeous grandma in the world. She must have carried me as a baby during every waking hour—since before I could even form memories. She must have kissed me and spanked me, the same way she had done with Hei Jian. She must have fed me breakfast near a bright, sunlit window on a beautiful day just like today.

## ❄ Chapter 6

I Wished for a White Christmas

I wished for a white Christmas, but ended up with a sunny and dry one. In the afternoon our school put on a Christmas play, performed entirely in English. I was cast in the role of the Big Bad Wolf.

"I am wery, WERRRY hungry!" I grumbled with a thick, slurred tongue in a throaty voice. My performance stirred up raucous laughter from the audience.

Jing beamed as she watched our play. When she laughed, she would hold a hand over her mouth. Jing has a beautiful set of teeth, but she liked to laugh with her hand covering her mouth.

I had told Jing about the Christmas play. Jie didn't know about it because I hadn't told her. I didn't want the two of them showing up together. I had a strange feeling that if Jie and Jing both came to the play, I would have a hard time deciding who to sit with. Sometimes, I felt closer to Jing than I did to Hei Jian, even after they had drifted apart.

Our teacher praised the play as a huge success. She also made a special mention of my performance, saying how having a dad in the movie industry is a big help. I didn't think it was a thing to be proud of. But a compliment is a compliment, so I was delighted to receive it.

I was secretly very happy to spot Jing in the hallway near the backstage entrance. She was wearing a light blue jacket and a fluffy white scarf. I wondered if she'd ever get bored of dressing that way.

After the show was over, Jing took me out. She wanted me to meet someone—the man we had talked about before. The meeting was going to take place over dinner. Grown-ups preferred to meet up at a restaurant while we students liked to hang out with our friends in a classroom.

To be honest, the guy and Jing were not a good match. I didn't like him one bit. I also didn't like the way Jing looked at him—as if she had completely forgotten about Hei Jian. Most of all, I detested the way he looked at Jing. As far as I know, only Hei Jian had ever looked at Jing that way, and the guy wasn't half as handsome as Hei

Jian. He had a balding head and didn't seem young at all. His teeth were crooked and a few of them were stained dark by tobacco smoke.

"You can call him Brother Quan," Jing said.

I felt a rush of relief. Calling him by that title meant that Jing hadn't yet decided to make their relationship official. And Quan called me "little buddy."

"Hey, little buddy, you gotta try this dish . . ." or "Eat some of that, little buddy." I didn't like it when strangers called me "buddy" or "kiddo." They sounded so condescending and made me feel stupid. Is a young person supposed to be dumber than an older person? The books I've read say that a person's IQ score doesn't change much after birth. So I've never believed that adults are smarter than us kids. They may be slyer than us, but that's only because they've had years to grow really good at telling half-truths.

When Jing told him that my name is Bai Jian, the guy immediately asked me about my dad. "So, what does Mr. Bai do for a living?"

I told him that my dad's name is actually Hei Jian, and that he plans to make a hit movie.

Quan paused for a second, then burst into laughter. "So your dad's name is Hei Jian . . . and you are Bai Jian? And he's going to be making a blockbuster movie? That's hilarious!"

I didn't smile. My pride was bruised. I turned toward Jing—she wasn't smiling either. She glared at Quan with a frown on her face. If Jing was upset, I couldn't possibly feel good either. Or maybe I was secretly glad, because that meant she wasn't completely over Hei Jian yet.

After dinner, Quan offered to take us for some fun activities, but Jing said, "No, I have to bring him back before the school gates close."

As they stood talking by the restaurant's doorway, I noticed that Quan wasn't very tall. In fact, he was shorter than Jing. I didn't bother watching them any longer. I turned around and started walking toward my school. I didn't slow down, even when Jing shouted after me.

She eventually caught up to me. She didn't ask why I hadn't waited for her. We slowed down our pace and strolled side by side.

"What do you think of him?" Jing asked.

"Not great," I replied.

"Why?"

At first, I didn't know how to answer her, so I kept quiet. Eventually I said, "I think he's a wiser guy than Hei Jian. He seems to know everything, except movies. And Hei Jian knows nothing except movies."

"Why does someone have to know how to make movies? Isn't being able to watch movies good enough?" she protested. "Besides, Quan is rich and he treats me well, unlike Hei Jian."

You don't have to explain your choice to me, I thought to myself, and I won't share what you said with Hei Jian. But I kept quiet. I felt like Jing was struggling to work through a math puzzle.

Suddenly, she seemed to have solved it. "It really is better for you to stay with your mom. And Hei Jian has already found a new girlfriend. There's just no need for me to stick around. You're all in your proper places. I can really disappear now. In the end, I was just a random bus stop along your life's journey. But I'm scared, Bai Jian . . . scared that I can't get used to anyone else but you and him."

I felt helpless and distraught. I didn't know what to say to make her feel better.

Wiping away tears, she said, "How silly of me, whining and complaining to a child." She sniffled. "Come. Let's sing a cheerful song. 'Jingle Bells, Jingle Bells . . .'" But her voice was not at all cheerful—it sounded like it would rather hide in a corner and cry. After a few lines, she broke down again and couldn't continue singing anymore.

We parted ways quietly in front of my school. Then back to my bustling dorm room I went, where I felt like a feather being dropped into a bubbling pot. All the unpleasantness of earlier that day, melted away without a trace.

To be honest, I liked the people in my dorm. Although there were eleven guys squeezed into a small space, and everyone's different: some were real airheads, some were smart but cocky, some shy and wishy-washy, some thick-skinned, . . . yet all were happy-go-lucky and easy to please. A sticker sheet or a stack of cards would delight them and keep them entertained for a long time.

I was known as "Prince Melancholy"—a nickname given to me by the girls in my class. But I had a difficult time staying melancholic in the dorm. Maybe I wasn't even melancholic by nature. Perhaps I had simply spent too much time brooding.

Tonight my dorm-mates were engaged in a simulated battle. The two-level bunk beds divided us into various camps and served as the perfect battlefield. We pretended we were starring in an action film, or a 007-style spy thriller. We threw our pillows like grenades. The bedsheets and blankets all turned into weapons too. You could be pretty aggressive without getting hurt.

We pulled off our bedsheets and spread them across the floor. A couple of my dorm-mates stood on top of them and wrestled around.

One guy dressed up as a girl by tying a blanket around his waist to make a skirt and tucking two buns under his sweater to make boobs. I laughed so hard I nearly fell on the floor. When they heard my laughter, one of them turned to me and said, "Bai Jian, why are you laughing so hard? This guy doesn't even look like a woman. Why don't you dress up instead?" They swarmed around me and tried to strip off my pants. I refused to let them and fought back tooth and nail.

I broke one guy's nose. Crimson-red blood spurted out, dripping down his face and smearing everywhere. He began to bawl. The game was over; we couldn't continue playing anymore. Everyone went back to bed, leaving the guy to cry alone.

I apologized to him—I didn't mean to hurt him. I tried to take him to the bathroom to wash it off, but he ducked out of my way and spat, "You're such a nasty person! We horsed around for a long time and nobody got hurt, but right after you came in, things got all rough and out of control. It's true what they say—motherless children are so wild!"

Blood rushed to my head and my heart pounded in my chest. I clenched my fist and demanded, "Who said that? Tell me!"

He looked scared. He stammered while covering his bloodied nose, "No . . . no one said it. That's just what I read in a book."

"Which book?"

Just then, the dorm parent arrived on scene, which was exactly what we had feared. That meant tomorrow morning, our head teacher would be informed of the incident and punishment was inescapable. In addition, they would probably have the dorm parent sleep on the same floor as us until we stopped causing mischief and learned to behave.

The dorm parent glared at me from the doorway. "Bai Jian, it's you again."

"I didn't hit him, my arm just happened to make contact with his face!" I protested.

The other guys were still milling around, so the dorm parent pointed at them and yelled, "Do you all know what time it is? Get to bed now!" Before I had opened my mouth to speak again, they had all fled back to their bunk beds, leaving me and the dorm parent staring into each other's faces under the ghostly pale light.

She was an old lady who always smelled like fried leek. A retired kindergarten teacher, she was a reasonable person who often reminded us to be considerate of others in communal life. "You should follow the rules of the system, and try to not act like spoiled little kings as if you're still living at home. Please, learn to be law-abiding citizens. It will do you much good."

I thought she was about to lecture me on rational reasoning and social etiquette again. But I was wrong. She didn't deliver such a speech. Instead, she asked me sternly, "What did your mother teach you about how to treat others?"

I didn't reply.

She raised her voice and asked again, "What did your mom teach you at home?"

I remained silent.

"Answer me!"

I hollered back, "Well, I don't have a mom!"

"What kind of attitude is that? How can you say that you don't have a mom? Who gave birth to you then? Do you know how sad your mom would be if she ever heard you say that?"

One guy spoke up quietly from his bunk bed. "Um, teacher, he doesn't have a mom because his mom abandoned him after giving birth."

"Shut the fuck up!" I shouted at him. I saw the dorm parent's mouth gape open in shock. Shame flooded me and made my eyes water. I turned around and ran outside.

Our school was located very close to a river. Without even thinking, I dashed toward the riverbank as fast as I could. I was usually scared of the shadowy bushes that lurked around there. As I slumped down near the edge of the river, fear—compounded by anger and shame—made me cry out loud. The sound of my wailing and sobbing echoed through the dark chambers of the night. Even the specks of light floating upon the surface of the river seemed to shiver as they heard my trembling voice. The scenery around me made me extra sad. Why did all these unhappy things have to happen to me? Why couldn't I ever get fair treatment?

The dorm parent came running after me. Swinging a flashlight, she called out my name as she scanned around. I hid behind a tree. When she didn't see me, she kept searching farther away. Suddenly, the idea of running away popped into my head. I knew that there were many boats cruising up and down the river. They would sail all the way up to Chongqing. I vaguely remembered that Hei Jian was originally from Chongqing. A woman gave birth to him in a hospital in Chongqing, and, soon afterward, my nainai took him home. He has been Nainai's son ever since.

I thought maybe I could hitch a ride to Chongqing on one of those boats and find Hei Jian's real mom for him. But how to find her whereabouts? I had no clue. I didn't know her name. I also didn't know much about Hei Jian's history before I was born. For the first time, I realized I didn't know as much about him as I had thought.

I heard the dorm parent returning. As she walked around where I was hiding, she shouted, "Bai Jian, where are you? Can you please come out? I'm sorry I wronged you. I apologize, okay? If you don't come back today and something happened to you, I will be in big trouble! I can't afford to lose my job. I have a sick husband to take care of, a son who just got laid off, and a grandchild who's going to school. If I can't work, my family will be ruined. I beg you, Bai Jian, please come out."

When I heard what she'd said, I felt really sorry for her. I remembered she was always wearing this faded sweater with threadbare cuffs. She also wore an old, patched-up cotton jacket the entire winter. On Monday it was clean and by Friday it would become visibly dusty and grimy. Then, the following Monday, it turned clean again. If she had enough money, wouldn't she have bought another jacket?

She was sobbing now. "Bai Jian, you've got to come out! If I have to call the police, you and I will both be doomed!"

I inched closer to the edge of the bush, within the path of the flashlight. She saw me. She stumbled over and gave me a hug. "You just about scared the dear old life out of me."

"I have one condition. And I won't go back with you unless you agree to it." I knew she would say yes to just about anything right now. "You must promise me that you won't tell any teacher about what happened tonight." She thought about it, then agreed.

If any of my teachers were to get wind of what happened, Hei Jian would eventually be informed. Hei Jian's reactions were unpredictable.

I had no idea what kind of punishment would be in store for me if he found out.

On the way back to the dorm, both of us kept our lips sealed. When we arrived, the dorm parent made me a cup of warm milk, which I drank quietly. Then I snuck under the covers.

The following day, Jing brought me some school supplies. I knew it was her excuse to come visit me. She smiled and asked, "Hey Bai Jian, your mom is pretty nice to you, right?"

I told her I didn't feel anything special in that regard. Everybody was pretty nice to me.

"Really? So who do you like the most?"

"No one," I said.

"Come on Bai Jian, be honest. You *must* like someone. Everyone's got a favorite person."

"Not me," I said.

"What about Hei Jian? Don't you like him?"

Honestly, to me, Hei Jian felt so distant and out of reach most of the time. Whenever I needed him or missed him, he was almost never around. And when he was close by, my need for him turned less urgent and pressing. It was so strange—I didn't know how to explain it. So I said nothing.

Jing suddenly looked me in the eye and said, "Bai Jian, I have an idea. If you don't end up staying with your mom, you can come stay with me. We'll start a new life together, okay?"

"Okay," I replied. "But what about Hei Jian?"

"He can live with his new girlfriend in a new home."

"What about Quan?"

"He will have his own life too."

"I don't know." I grinned. "You grown-ups can decide this kind of stuff on your own."

"Well, I have decided that I'm going to live with you for the rest of my life. You will be my son and I will be your mom," she declared. "You don't have to call me mom. You can continue to call me Jing. Our little home will be warm and cozy. I'll send you to a nice college so you can get a solid education. You will be my pride and joy."

That night, Jing also invited me to spend New Year's Eve with her. She wanted to visit Hainan Island for Lunar New Year. We would fly there on a plane and hang out on the beach all day, enjoying the waves, sand, and vibrant festivities. "I don't think you have ever been on an airplane," Jing finished.

Her description of the vacation really tempted me. It brought back fond memories of the time we used to live together, when Jing had really felt like my mom with her warm and stern presence. I wanted to feel those feelings again. Plus, I hadn't visited the ocean before either. Who wouldn't want to see a real ocean? "Well, you would have to run it by Hei Jian first," I answered.

"Of course. But I don't see any reason why he would object."

Before Jing came to see me, I had been playing basketball with some students. I was playing center. While we were speaking, my teammates stood around the court, waiting for me to return to the game and pass the ball. I had to end my conversation with Jing. So I told her yes, we should go on a vacation to Hainan.

When I got back to the game and was about to take a shot, I thought, Was Jing really serious about what she said? Maybe she spoke to me about those things because she missed Hei Jian too much.

I couldn't be sure. Eventually, I had to let go of those thoughts and focus back on the game.

A little bit later, I thought, Jing is such a nice person, and she looks so compatible with Hei Jian. Why did Hei Jian have to break up with her? That was one of the things I couldn't figure out about grown-ups. I even went as far as thinking that if Hei Jian truly cared about me, he would marry Jing and the three of us would live under one roof. As a family, we would get up together and eat at regular times every day. But I knew Hei Jian wouldn't do that. He wouldn't inconvenience his life, just for my sake.

## Chapter 7

### The Fall Semester Ended in a Whiteout Snowstorm

The fall semester ended in a whiteout snowstorm. On the second-to-last day of the semester, without warning, Hei Jian turned up at my school looking all dusty and worn. He had grown a bushy beard and sported a red puffy down jacket, as if he'd just returned from a ski trip.

As soon as Hei Jian spotted me, and without saying a word, he lifted me into the air. Then he pounced into my dorm room and rushed around trying to help me pack.

"Where are we headed?" I asked.

"Just come with me," he said without looking up.

Since Hei Jian was still in a good mood at this point, I wanted to clear up something with him. I pressed on. "Where exactly are we going?"

"Wherever I'm going, you are coming with me."

"But I have to know exactly where we're headed."

"Oh come on, just follow me! Do you think I will abduct you?"

I reminded him: "Jie asked me to spend New Year's Eve with her. Jing also asked me."

Hei Jian stopped packing momentarily and stared at me. "So where do you want to go for New Year's Eve?"

I shook my head. I really didn't know. But since both of them had invited me, it seemed kind of rude if I were to leave without giving them a firm answer.

Hei Jian threw down the bag he was packing and said, "They've really gotten you wrapped around their little finger, haven't they?"

I shook my head again.

Hei Jian looked at me for a while, then barked, "Don't just stand here. Come and help me pack up your mess. We're leaving in an hour."

I inched away slowly. I had to go make some phone calls, so there wouldn't be two women showing up the very next day trying to pick me up from school. They'd probably be upset or sad if I just skipped out. It didn't matter to Hei Jian—he didn't have to face them. But I couldn't dodge them for long.

"Why are you dawdling?" Hei Jian demanded. "Come over here and hold this thing up for me." He wasn't good at packing. After going at it for a while, there was still a giant mess of stuff spread out on my bed.

I waited until Hei Jian had gone to the bathroom, then dashed into the front reception of the dorm. I told Grandpa Lu, who was on evening duty, "If a lady comes here asking for me, please tell her that I've already left with my dad."

"Wait, how old are you?" he asked. "You're already courting women?" (Grandpa Lu is a bit of an old perv.)

I didn't have time to explain things to him because Hei Jian was coming back soon.

Thirty minutes later we boarded the bus. Right before we got on, Hei Jian pulled me aside to comb out my hair. He also spritzed a generous amount of hairspray on my head and straightened out my shirt collar. As soon as he did that, I knew I was about to meet a new auntie. It's part of Hei Jian's strategy to help keep up appearances. I was like a piece of clothing being shown off to prop up his image. He was always so picky about what he wore, just like how he was always particular about maintaining his image.

I saw my own reflection on the bus window. I hated the way I looked: hair neatly combed back, sleek and tame; mouth flushed pink like a girl's; eyes beaming brightly like a pair of light bulbs; face unbelievably pale. I finally understood why those guys at school called me Jia Baoyu, a girly wimp. Earlier in the school year, I had tried to make myself look rougher around the edges by not washing or grooming for several days in a row. But instead of the result I wanted, all I got was a big scolding from my guidance counselor.

I noticed Hei Jian peering over at me. Grinning, he said, "That boarding school must be a nice place. They've got you looking healthy and vigorous—plump cheeks and some color in your face. If you had stayed with me, you would be starved down to your bones."

Just as I had expected, there was a woman waiting for us at the bus terminal. I didn't need Hei Jian to remind me; I already knew how to behave in this situation. I walked up to her, smiled sweetly, and said, "Hello, Auntie!" I could tell that she was impressed by the manner I greeted her, because she gushed with exaggerated enthusiasm, "My goodness, Hei Jian! I didn't expect your son to be so big already. He's almost taller than me! And he's so handsome."

Hei Jian introduced her. Her name was Wei.

Then we went out to eat at a restaurant, where a waiter served us at our private table. I could tell that Wei was financially very well off. She asked me to order some food, so I obliged by ordering a super expensive shrimp dish. That's one of the things Hei Jian taught me: people judge a person's standard of living and personal taste based on the type of food they order. I didn't want to make Hei Jian look bad. Sure enough, Wei looked pleased. She said to Hei Jian, "You raised your son well all by yourself. I appreciate a man like that—one with a great sense of responsibility."

I held my tongue.

For the rest of the meal, they pretty much just talked to each other. Only occasionally, when they remembered that I was still there, did they offer to grab me some food or refill my cup. Eating was such a boring activity, especially when it was with Hei Jian and his girl-friend. They would get lost in their own conversations and treat me like I was invisible. Or else things went along fine until they would suddenly—and mysteriously—blow up, and they would part ways on bad terms.

At some point, the conversation at the table landed on the topic of the Lunar New Year.

"Let's head northeast," Wei said. "We can experience a real winter in Dongbei."

"That's too extravagant," Hei Jian said.

"Oh, don't worry about that. Besides, I've worked hard all year. I deserve a nice holiday trip."

"That has nothing to do with me though. If you want to give yourself a nice vacation, just go by yourself."

"But you're coming with me! You have to! That's my New Year's present to myself."

"Oh, so I'm a gift you give to yourself? No way then."

"No need to put it so bluntly like that. Even if it was true, why am I only inviting you and no one else?" Wei asked. "Please come! Let's spend New Year's together. Let's go get lost under a thick blanket of ice and snow!"

"Don't tempt me, okay?" Hei Jian chuckled. "You know, my greatest weakness is not being able to say no to people." Then he pretended to half-heartedly accept Wei's invitation, while I cringed with embarrassment on his behalf. But I couldn't interfere with his plans. I could only sit there and accept his orders. Nobody bothered to ask for my opinion or thoughts. Up until the moment we finished the meal and left the table, neither of them cared to ask, *Hey Bai Jian, would you like to come to Dongbei with us for New Year's?*

Of course, a trip up north was very tempting. I heard that the snowflakes there were as big as a person's fist, and they didn't melt when they landed on the ground. I was very curious to see that kind of snow. But I decided not to get on their case.

With a wave of her hand, Wei summoned the waiter, who walked over and respectfully presented her with the bill. With a graceful flick of her perfectly manicured fingers, a stack of large bills flew out of her wallet, swirled through the air, and headed straight into the waiter's hand.

After dinner—no surprise—we went shopping. "Hey Bai Jian, I want to give you a New Year's present," Wei announced. Like clockwork. Then she led us into a children's clothing store, not bothering to see if I wanted something else. It's just like what I said: Jie, Jing, and all the aunties I've met only thought of buying me more clothes. I had enough clothes to wear. The thing that I really wanted? A language-learning machine. Most of the students in my class owned one, and every time I had to borrow it from them they'd say, "But you have so many fancy outfits! Why don't you use the money you'd spend on clothes to get yourself some school supplies?"

Those words made me feel so ashamed of myself. They made me sound like a dandy who only cared for fine foods and clothing and who didn't like to study.

I shook my head at every piece of clothing Wei and Hei Jian picked out for me, and eventually they started to look exasperated. Then I pretended to casually stroll toward the stationary aisle, finally stopping in front of a display of language-learning machines. Hei Jian clued in. He said, "Hey Bai Jian, why don't I get you a present for the New Year too? What would you like?"

"I need a machine to help me learn English."

Hei Jian took one look at the price and said, "No way! That's too expensive. Let's go somewhere else. They mark things up so much here."

Wei really fell for it. She looked at the price tag and said, "Oh, that's not expensive at all. If you're going to buy something, you should go for quality. Get a nice brand or it won't work properly." She turned to ask the store clerk, "Do you have one that's even better quality?" After being reassured this product was the best the store carried, she pulled out her wallet.

I felt kind of bad about what I was doing, but I did really want that machine. I knew Hei Jian would never buy me something like that. He would always tell me, "Don't trust those glossy commercials. Learning is all about finishing your homework and preparing well for your exams. Don't get too fancy. The best learning machines are not half as good as a smart and hardworking brain. Those ad developers have ways of tricking people into buying useless stuff." Hei Jian said that as someone who had worked in the advertising field; he didn't want other people to use those underhanded tactics to cheat his son. I couldn't counter him. Hei Jian always deployed so many "logical arguments" to discourage me from spending money; he had probably squeezed dry all his brain juices coming up with these arguments.

After we finished shopping, we went to Wei's place, a luxurious-looking condo with three bathrooms. I thought Wei would let me stay in one of the bedrooms for the night. But instead, she started fixing up the living room couch for me to sleep.

Hei Jian asked, "Why not let him sleep on a bed? The living room is so empty. It's no fun catching a cold."

But Wei said, "Oh, he should be fine sleeping on the couch for a couple of days. Besides, it's a big hassle to have to clean up an entire bedroom."

Just two days? I had over twenty days of holiday break left. Slowly, I began to suspect that there was something more going on beneath the surface. I glanced over at Hei Jian. He didn't look bothered at all. Maybe I was being too sensitive.

The next morning, Wei woke me up with a smile on her face. I sat down at the breakfast table by the window. There was freshly baked bread and gently steaming milk—both of which smelled heavenly—plus many other tasty items. I beamed from the bottom of my heart.

"Bai Jian, I love your smile," Wei said. "You look even more like Hei Jian when you smile."

The lucky dude had just woken up. His hair was meticulously combed, and he was actually wearing a brown bathrobe. Everybody seemed to be in a good mood. Wei looked at Hei Jian, then at me, and exclaimed, "What a sweet scene this is!"

"You know, you can keep it forever if you like." Hei Jian nudged her.

Wei smiled. "I've always enjoyed looking at beautiful scenes, whether they come from a movie or from real life."

"So you like them in the most superficial way," Hei Jian said.

Wei burst out laughing. "Oh Hei Jian, it's so fun to be around you. You always know how to hit my weak spots. You know, you have put me under a curse. You're cursing me to stay alone, to never grasp the happiness I want!" After that, Wei's mood took a nosedive. For the rest of the meal, she barely spoke and didn't look in my direction at all. When breakfast was finished, we went out together. We planned to visit an amusement park and take some pictures, then go see a movie.

But before we got started on any of the fun group activities, our good mood was completely destroyed by what took place in front of the travel agency.

It started with Hei Jian pointing it out to Wei. "Look, that's your dream Dongbei vacation right there!"

Wei said, "That reminds me, we need to book our tickets." So in they went to buy their tickets.

About ten minutes later, they exited the building with Hei Jian walking ahead. Hei Jian's face was dark and grim. He came over, grabbed my shoulder, and said in a stern voice, "Let's go!" leaving Wei trailing behind us.

As I trotted beside him, I asked, "Hey, Hei Jian, did you guys argue? Why are you always getting into arguments with women?"

Hei Jian pinched me hard and barked, "Shut your mouth!"

Wei strode up to us and protested, "Like you heard, they've only got two tickets left."

"Cut that crap," Hei Jian replied. "Just fess up—you don't want Bai Jian to come along, so you made up some shitty excuse. You just want to camp out in a remote place where there's nobody but you and your man, so you can get wasted. Why don't you just say that? I can accept that. But don't try to pull the wool over my eyes with some pretentious bullshit."

"Okay, you want facts? I'll give you the facts, straight up," Wei snapped. "I hate other people's kids. My own child is still under the control of my ex-husband and getting tortured by his fucking bitch of a wife. Why do I have to butter up someone else's kid? Even looking at this boy rips open my old wounds."

Then she began to sob. "I couldn't buy my own son a present for the holidays, and I couldn't take him on a vacation. So if I let Bai Jian join us on this trip, I would feel like my son was watching over my shoulders and fuming at me. Do you understand?"

Wei stood trembling in the middle of the street, drenched in tears. Her face was a streaky mess of black and red. Hei Jian clenched his jaw and listened to her cry for a while. Then he abruptly walked over, pulled her into his arms, and said, "It's okay, let's go home. Let's forget all our worries. Just pack our bags and get ready to go to Dongbei."

Wei said, "Hei Jian, let's go home. But we're not going to Dongbei. What's so special about that place? What do we expect to find there?"

Hei Jian was being stubborn now. He insisted that they go. "I don't want you to spend the entire next year nagging about how you had missed your northern vacation because of me."

"I won't. Promise. I'll forget all about it in a second."

"Yeah right, bullshit. You won't be able to forget."

"Then, maybe we can take Bai Jian along?"

"No, he's not coming. He's got another place to go."

Later on, Hei Jian took me to see a movie while Wei stayed home to make dinner. I knew right away that he wanted to talk with me. So I said, "Hei Jian, just let me leave."

"Are you kidding? Where do you think you're going?"

In moments like this, I would remember Hei Jian always telling me, "Bai Jian, I have to give you a home and a family of our own." This usually happened after he had just broken up with an auntie. He and

I would wrap our arms around each other and wade through an ocean of people like a pair of drowning brothers, clinging to each other for dear life.

But as soon as he had gotten out of that slump, Hei Jian would quickly forget what he had said to me. Right now, I desperately hoped that he would make what he had promised a reality. If we lived in our own home, we wouldn't have to be so watchful and vigilant of other people's whims and wishes. We could sleep in whenever we liked and chill out to our hearts' content. But when would we ever have a home like that?

"Can I go back to Jie?" I asked Hei Jian, fully expecting him to jump up and object vehemently like he had before.

He didn't reply right away. Then, finally, he said, "Tell me the truth. Do you really wish to stay with her?"

I couldn't say yes, because that wasn't my heart's true desire. But I couldn't say no either, because that would have made Hei Jian's situation more difficult. So I weighed everything very carefully before responding. I said that I should at least spend New Year's Eve with Jie, since she had given birth to me.

"Bai Jian, you have really grown up." Hei Jian breathed a long sigh of relief.

I knew Hei Jian had approved my plan. But after confirming this with him, I felt even more sad and lost. If I was really honest with myself, I much preferred staying with Hei Jian than with anyone else. But he had his own life. If I was constantly dragging him down or getting in his way, he would quickly grow sick and tired of me. So, instead of having people be sick of you, it was better to sacrifice your own interests and make people feel sorry for you. That's a lesson I've learned from living with Hei Jian.

We went to see the new *Harry Potter*, a movie that made me feel even more melancholic. How I wished I could go to a wizarding school too. Since nobody could help me solve all my problems, maybe magic could?

Hei Jian repeated those words again, "Bai Jian, next year—no, this year—I'll for sure get you a home. We'll never have to think about where to spend New Year's again. We'll spend it in our own home."

"You keep saying those words, year after year, but nothing ever happens!"

Hei Jian sighed. "When you grow up, you'll see that it's not easy to build a home that you like. You need money, but you also need affection in your home. Both things are hard to come by. Sometimes, even when you manage to find both, they can slip away. Or become spoiled with time. Do you understand what I'm saying?"

"Yes," I said. "I get it." How could I not?

Hei Jian slapped my head and said, "Bullshit. I'd be scared if you actually understood it."

There was only one day left until New Year's Eve. I picked up my bags and set off on my journey back to school. Hei Jian and Wei buzzed around me, trying to attend to all my needs. I could tell they were starting to regret their decision. They felt guilty. Several times, they were on the verge of changing their minds. But I didn't give them the chance to backtrack. I wanted that guilt to grow and deepen—to sink into their bones. I sprinted ahead like a grown-up person in a rush to get somewhere, while they trailed behind me, scurrying along like two panicked children. As I strode on, I cursed them in my heart. Go to hell! GO TO HELL!!

When my bus drove off, I saw Hei Jian standing there, body stiff and face darkened like a real black key piece. Wei, on the other hand, stood a step away from him and continuously waved at me. I didn't bother to wave back. I just stared at Hei Jian the entire time, unblinking.

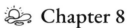 **Chapter 8**

New Year's Eve was Going to be Nice and Sunny

The weather forecast said that New Year's Eve was going to be a nice and sunny day. I arrived at Jie's place the afternoon before New Year's Eve. The slanting sun pulled my shadow into the shape of a long, slender bamboo stick. I knocked on her door but no one answered. Maybe she was out shopping or taking a stroll. Two hours passed, then three. Still, no one opened the door. I had no choice but to head over to Jie's relative's place. I had gone there with Jie before, so

I figured she would know Jie's whereabouts. Jie wasn't there though, and the old lady told me with a coy smile on her face that Jie had gone to Uncle Li's home for New Year's Eve. My heart started to churn with panic. I forced myself to calm down.

"May I use your phone to call Jie?"

She dialed a number and passed me the handset. Jie's voice rang distant and hollow from the other side. She said, "I went to pick you up at your school the day before the holiday break started, but they told me you had already left with Hei Jian."

"When are you coming back?" I asked hurriedly.

"Oh, I'm in a different province right now. Be a good boy and behave yourself when you're with Hei Jian, okay?" She didn't even ask if I was physically with Hei Jian. "Hey, wanna talk to Uncle Li? I'm here visiting his hometown."

"No." I hastily hung up the phone and dashed out the door.

The old lady chased after me. "Where are you going, Bai Jian?"

I replied as I ran, "I'm going home." I headed toward a home that existed only in my mind. And I was tired of running. I stopped by the side of the road. My head was trembling from inside. I saw a middle-aged couple emerge from a nearby supermarket. They carried a few large grocery bags and looked content. While I stared at them, an idea popped into my head: I should get married as early as possible. After getting married, I would have my own home—a quiet and comfortable place where I could lie down to rest undisturbed whenever I wanted. Seriously, I couldn't wait, even though I was barely twelve years old.

After walking for a while, I found myself at Jing's doorstep. I thought, why not spend New Year's Eve at her place? She had invited me a while back; she had also told me that she was willing to live with me for the rest of her life. Even before I knocked, I felt an aura of warmth emenating through the door. The door itself was an earthy brick red—the warmest hue in the world. Just as I raised my hand to knock, the door popped open, startling the people standing on either side of it.

It was Brother Quan who opened the door. He rubbed his hand on his chest and kept muttering, "Oh, you nearly scared me to death! You really scared me . . ."

Jing peeked her head out from behind Quan. "Bai Jian, why are you here?"

I put on a smile, unable to answer her for a moment. She pulled me aside and asked me where Hei Jian was. I tried to hold back my tears.

"Tell me, where's Hei Jian? Did something happen to him?"

I told her he was leaving for Dongbei to vacation with Wei. Jing loosened her grip on my arm. Her face turned pale and her hands began to tremble. She said, "Are you sure that woman's name is Wei?" I nodded. "Do they live together now?" I nodded again. "So he was cheating on me after all. He denied it back when we broke up. Why did he cheat? Is he really as heartless as they say? A man without an ounce of morals . . . ?" She stood up, mumbling to herself. Her gaze was scattered, confused.

I noticed that the two of them had luggage. There were two large suitcases near Quan's feet.

"Hurry up, we will miss the last train if we don't get going now."

Jing was still talking to herself. "I must never think of him again . . . that heartless man. I despise him! I can't let things keep going like this. Never again!" She drifted toward Quan as if she had fallen into a trance and reached for his hand like a lost ghost. Then she said, "Let's go. From now on, I will follow you wherever you go."

Quan held her hand. "Silly. Who else would you follow if not your husband-to-be?"

Jing seemed to have completely forgotten about my existence. Quan looked at me and then at her. In the urgency of the moment, an idea came to me. "Hey, why don't you guys just head out. I need to use the bathroom. I'll lock the door behind me when I leave, okay?"

"Okay," Jing answered absent-mindedly. As I dove into the bathroom, I heard the sound of the front door closing. Then the door reopened, and Quan peeked his head in. "Hey Bai Jian, really make sure you lock the front door when you leave."

"Okay, I will!" I shouted. He shut the door. Then, the tears that I had been fighting back finally flowed free. I tried to wipe them away. On the eve of the Lunar New Year, the biggest holiday of the year, I was alone.

I had to find a way to keep going, to take care of myself even when I was all by myself.

"Damn you all! You promised to spend New Year's with me, but you all forgot what you said! Go to hell, Jie. Go to hell, Jing. Go to hell, Wei. Go to hell, Hei Jian and all your women! Everybody, why don't you all go to hell?! I don't need any of you! I can spend the New Year on my own. No need for a mom or dad."

When I was done venting, I emptied my schoolbag and grabbed my winter workbook. Homework. The first thing I needed to do was to finish my homework, just like the students whose parents were around. Next, I would head out to the supermarket to buy some food.

Luckily, Hei Jian had tossed me some change before we parted ways. I planned to buy instant noodles, snacks, milk, and maybe some fruit. Then I would try to figure out what else I needed for New Year's Eve. Oh, I wanted to get some books. I loved reading comics. Finally, there was nobody around to stop me from buying those comic books. I could read my favorite ones to my heart's content. In fact, I could do whatever I wanted. I was in charge of my own life. The very thought made my heart thump suddenly with excitement.

Perhaps spending New Year's alone wasn't such a bad thing after all. I thought back to that time when Jing, Hei Jian, and I spent the New Year together. Jing argued with him for almost the entire holiday break because Hei Jian took a call from another woman. It wasn't until the day before Jing had to return to work that she and Hei Jian finally made up. Caught in the middle of all that, I got so stressed out. It was torturous. At least this year I wouldn't have to experience anything like that.

I planned to go play video games at an internet cafe too. I hadn't played that stuff in a long time. Who would care if I played video games or not? Nobody was around to judge me.

I carried out my plans diligently and meticulously:

In the evening, I watched the annual Spring Festival Gala on TV. The programming was dull as usual—I fell asleep while watching. When I woke up, it was the morning of the New Year.

I ate a bit of breakfast and started to do more homework. It didn't take long for me to feel bored. I just couldn't focus on the homework any longer. I wanted to head out to play some video games. I balled up a piece of paper and stuck it into the hole of the lock so I wouldn't accidentally lock myself out when I closed the front door.

The internet cafe was bustling and crowded. The busy tapping of keyboards sounded like raindrops pounding away endlessly. The sights and sounds of the place stirred up a wave of joyous excitement in my chest. This was the true spirit and festive mood of Lunar New Year. I hurried inside and found an empty spot to sit down. Happiness instantly hugged me like a warm blanket.

I heard a boy sitting next to me hang up his cell phone and whine, "So annoying. She keeps calling me and telling me to go home. I've only played like two rounds."

"Yeah. Orphans are really the lucky ones," chimed his friend. "They don't have anyone looking over their shoulders all the time. They're free to do whatever they want."

I glanced over at them and smirked.

I ended up spending the next three days inside the internet cafe. What a blast! If I hadn't gotten so hungry and bleary-eyed, I would have kept on playing.

After the third day, I walked into a tiny, hole-in-the-wall dumpling house and scarfed down two large bowls of dumplings. By the time I got back to Jing's place, my belly was bloated. As soon as I got in, I dropped down and fell asleep. When I woke up again, I was so disoriented at first, I didn't know what day it was. I started to tackle my homework more seriously.

We had all been given a workbook to be completed over the winter break. We had to write an essay on "My Fun Winter Vacation." I thought about it and wrote down this:

*Is it possible for a person to have no mom? Impossible. Unless that mom abandons you.*

*Is it possible for a person to have no dad? Impossible, unless that father doesn't want you.*

*Is it possible for a person to skip New Year's Eve? Impossible. Unless you can rip that page out of the calendar.*

*If your mom leaves you, your dad doesn't want you, and the Earth won't allow you to skip a day just because you don't like it, how do you get on?*

*I want to give you some advice based on my own experience.*

*So what if your mom leaves? So what if your dad's never around? As long as you are still breathing—as long as you wish to be happy—you can still have a totally kick-ass New Year! Even if there's no New Year's Eve family feast, no presents or red envelopes to open, and no firecrackers to light, you can still find joy. You can still make yourself happy.*

This was the introduction I wrote for my essay. It sounded a little familiar, like the opening act of a certain novel that someone else had written. But I didn't care. I was resolved, more than ever before, to take control of my life and future, starting that very day.

# ⚒ Chapter 9

### The Weather Turned Crappy on the Sixth Day of New Year

On the sixth day of the Lunar New Year, the weather suddenly turned crappy. The sky became gloomy and dark early in the morning. A blustery wind swept through town. I accidentally touched the lamp at the head of Jing's bed and it came alive and started to blast music loudly. It was a radio alarm lamp. On the radio, the host of the station announced that today was the sixth day of the new year and

the last day of the public holiday period. When I realized that my winter break was nearly over and I had to leave, I felt kind of sad. Jing was
coming home today, or tomorrow at the latest, because she had to go
back to work. She must not know that I had been hiding in her place
all this time.

Where could I go instead? Jie probably hadn't returned yet,
because she didn't need to work. Even if she had already come back
into town, she would probably be hanging around Uncle Li like his
shadow. I didn't like that guy one bit. And he probably felt the same
way about me. Why would I go there and subject myself to their surly
scowls? Hei Jian must be up in Dongbei still. I vaguely remembered
hearing him say that it was the only region in our amazingly vast
country that he hadn't yet visited. So he was likely going to stay there
for a good while, exploring every corner before returning home.
Maybe by the time he was ready to come back the spring would
be over.

I laid in bed and pondered all of this. Before I could come up with
a solid plan, I fell asleep. Next thing I knew, I was startled awake by
some kind of noise. When I opened my eyes, Jing was standing right
next to me. Her mouth was wide and gaping, like she had just seen a
ghost.

"Why are you here? How did you get in? I don't remember giving
you the keys to my place!" she blurted.

"When I came to visit you, you opened the door for me yourself.
Remember? That day when you left with Quan." I jumped out of bed
and tried to smile and look less awkward.

"You mean, you spent your entire winter break at my place?!"

I nodded.

"So you didn't go visit your mom? You were here all by yourself?"
I nodded again.

Jing turned away and faced the wall. I knew she was crying. She cried so easily.

"I'm sorry. I didn't ask for your permission first. But I was very careful—I didn't damage anything in your home."

She turned around, opened her arms, and hugged me as rivers of tears flowed down her cheeks. "What did you eat all these days? There's no food inside my home! How did you survive? Why didn't you tell me the truth that day? If I knew you had nowhere to go, I wouldn't have left. I'd have stayed with you, and we'd have spent the New Year together! It would have been so much better."

I didn't want to bring up all the unhappy stuff that had happened between Hei Jian and his girlfriend Wei and me. Plus, it wasn't so bad to have spent the holidays alone. I had finished nearly all my homework. And there were still three or four days left. Of course, I didn't tell her about my trip to the internet cafe. She would have cried even harder.

"Bai Jian, I think I'll ask for your parents' permission to adopt you. Wait, I'm sorry. I should ask you first. Would you like to live with me? Do you want me to be your mom? . . . Never mind, I don't think Brother Quan will approve."

What did any of that have to do with him? I was about to say something when Jing's phone rang.

"Yes, I'm home now. No, don't come over, I'm about to leave. No, no, it's nothing. I just want to go out to shop for a bit by myself. Dinner another time. Let's just do our own thing today, okay? Bye."

I knew it was Quan who had called. And Jing had just lied to him.

"Do you plan to take me out for dinner?" I asked.

"Of course. Let's go grab something delicious." She patted her purse. That purse had fattened up quite a bit since the holidays. "Today, you get to pick whatever food you like."

I was definitely ready to feast. I had gotten so tired of eating instant noodles. The very sight of them made me want to throw up.

We went to the Five Continental Restaurant Hotel. Hei Jian, Jing, and I had come here once before. Hei Jian had hosted us last time. After drowning in debt for a long stretch of time, he had suddenly received a large lump sum payment.

Back then, Jing had asked, "Why are we coming here to eat?" And Hei Jian had replied, "Why not? I've got money now. See, it's not that hard to earn some cash." Maybe he shouldn't have gloated like that, because soon after that, we went through our biggest drought ever, lasting a whole six months. Hei Jian lost all sources of income during that period, and had difficulty covering even our basic expenses.

The towering hotel was still decked out in the festive colors of the Lunar New Year. However, there weren't as many guests inside its restaurant or boutiques as when we were here last. This time, Jing didn't even pick up her chopsticks to eat. She just stared at me, watching me devour a full table of yummy food.

"Bai Jian, I want to ask you something," Jing said as I piled more food on my plate. "Do you think Wei is pretty?"

"Oh, she's just average." I knew she would ask me this, sooner or later. Seemed like Jing still hadn't made up her mind. She was still stuck thinking about the same things from before the New Year.

"You are not telling me the truth. I heard that Wei is very pretty."

"But *I* don't think she's all that pretty. She likes to wear fancy, expensive clothes, so that sort of prettiness is really a reflection of her fashion sense. She's not a naturally beautiful person." All the dishes were so tasty that I instinctively wanted to say things that would please Jing. "Even if Wei is pretty, she is also a bit stuck up. Not a very likeable person."

Jing still looked crestfallen. "Well, she has money. When a person has lots of money, nothing is a problem. What do you think—will she and Hei Jian get married?"

"No. Definitely not!" I answered with confidence. But of course, I wasn't sure. I was just bluffing. After all, how could I know if they were going to get married? Even Hei Jian himself probably didn't know.

"I know you're just trying to comfort me. They probably planned on getting married during their trip. Otherwise, why didn't they take you along? They must be going on their honeymoon now . . ." Jing did not continue. She propped her head up with her arms. Her legs dangled from the edge of her chair. Her face looked sullen, distraught.

I figured I'd better put down my chopsticks and tell her that I was already full. But I couldn't. My hands had a stubborn mind of their own. They rebelled against me and continued to reach for more food. The chefs here were amazing. Everything they cooked was out of this world.

On the way back, Jing pulled down the rim of her cotton sunhat. She also covered herself up even though the weather wasn't super cold. I think she just wanted to avoid interacting with me. It was her way of saying "leave me alone." So I walked behind her gingerly.

Suddenly, I realized something: Jing's clothes were black. She was no longer wearing only blue. She must have been trying to change herself—to transform.

When we got back, she made a bed for me on the floor of her room, then murmured, "Go to sleep."

In the middle of the night, we were both startled awake by the sound of loud, irritated knocking on the door.

Jing turned on the light and hopped out of bed. "Who is it?"

"Me!" It was Hei Jian.

Jing nearly sprinted to the door. Before she unlocked it, she paused. She smoothed out her hair and patted her face. Then she opened the door gently. "Why are you here? Aren't you supposed to be in Dongbei?"

Hei Jian didn't reply. He gave her a hug and walked over to where I was. "I knew you'd be here!" He hugged me, then pushed me away from his body. He squeezed my face, slapped my back, and pinched my ears. "I missed you so much," he told me as he stared at me. "Tell me, what did you do on New Year's Eve? Did you light some firecrackers?"

Jing said nothing. I was silent too.

"Let me guess, you didn't play with firecrackers because the two of you are such sissies. That's alright, I'm going to get you some tomorrow, to make it up to you! And thank you," Hei Jian said, looking at Jing, then back at me. "Now you know who's the best, right? Not me, or your mom. It's Jing. She takes the best care of you."

"Actually, you don't need to thank me." Jing seemed a bit embarrassed. Then she added, "I didn't spend the New Year with him. He spent it here alone."

"Is that true, my boy?" Hei Jian stared at me with a serious, almost scary expression. I lowered my eyes and squirmed. "So you were by yourself for seven whole days? Why didn't you stay with Jie? She's your mom. You told me you were going to her place after we parted."

"I did go. But she was out of town with her boyfriend," I whimpered.

Hei Jian pulled me into his arms again. "What did you eat these seven days?"

"I used some of the money you gave me to buy instant noodles. At first, I was worried that seven days were going to feel like an eternity. But time flew fast—that week went by in the blink of an eye."

Hei Jian lit up a cigarette. In seconds the entire apartment reeked.

"Nice. Great! Everybody's becoming so bold and independent." He snuffed out the cigarette, stood up, and said, "Let's go, son. We're checking into a hotel."

"What do you mean?" Jing interrupted. "He was sleeping here just fine." I was very familiar with Jing's body language. Every time before Jing and Hei Jian started to fight, she would look like she did now.

"I don't want to disturb you. You carry on, okay?" Hei Jian dragged me toward the bedroom door, ignoring my kicking and screaming.

"You jerk. What right do you have to be upset at me? Who am I to you? And why am I supposed to take care of him?"

"Fine. I don't have the right to be mad at you. You're not my someone. You have no duty of care toward him. But he has intruded into your home and disrupted your life for the past week. I apologize on his behalf," Hei Jian snarked. "Did you damage anything here, son?"

I wriggled out of his grasp and ducked out of the room. I didn't want to get caught in the brewing storm.

Fortunately, that day neither of them was in the mood for a big argument. Hei Jian simply slung my schoolbag over his shoulder and bolted out the door as Jing slid down next to her bed, looking dejected. I followed Hei Jian out.

"Hey Hei Jian, you really shouldn't have been so harsh on Jing. She didn't know I was hiding at her place. She only found out when she came home this morning." I proceeded to tell him how I managed to smuggle myself into Jing's home.

"I was wrong then. I blamed her by mistake," Hei Jian said. "But there's nothing I can do now. I can't take back what I said."

When we arrived at the hotel, I asked him, "How was Dongbei?"

"Just so-so. Nothing special. Definitely not as nice as I had imagined."

"What about Wei? Did you fight with her again? Jing said you guys went there to get married. Is that true?"

"Nonsense! How's that even possible? If I had planned to get married, I would have first come to you to ask for your permission!" he blurted.

That was the nicest thing I'd heard all night . . . no, the whole year. My mood turned bright and cheery all of a sudden. I told Hei Jian, "You know, if you really want to marry Wei, that's fine with me. She seems very capable. A woman like her can be very good for you."

"Never mind. I don't want to talk about it right now. Maybe I'll tell you later," he said. "Let's not forget the fact that you hid yourself inside someone else's home and spent seven days on your own. Had I known this, I would not have gone anywhere. I would have stayed with you so we could celebrate New Year's together." He looked remorseful.

It wasn't until many days later that Hei Jian finally told me what really happened during his vacation trip. The day after I left them, on New Year's Eve, he started to argue with Wei over something very trivial. As their argument continued, things turned ugly. Eventually, Wei threw out his things and told him to leave the hotel. Hei Jian was so humiliated, he slapped Wei in the face, twice. Then they got into a physical fight, and she called the police. The cops took Hei Jian away. He was kept in a detention cell at the police station until the day after New Year's, and only got released when all the officers went home for the holidays. After leaving the police station, he had no money on him and nowhere to stay, so he went back to Wei.

Hei Jian thought that Wei would be like his other ex-girlfriends— that they could patch things up quickly and easily after a big fight. But he was sorely mistaken. Wei was not like the women he had dated before. As soon as she saw him approaching her hotel suite, she locked the door and shut the windows. He stood outside her window in the chilly winter draft, shivering, calling out to her repeatedly. She refused to even look in his direction. She turned on her stereo speakers and blasted music at full volume. Then she began to groove to the rhythm and beat of the songs.

"You know, there's no warm place in this world. Everywhere you go, it's cold as hell," Hei Jian complained bitterly. For the first time since I could remember, he looked defeated.

"There are places that may be warm, but they come at a price. You have to give up something first in order to gain entrance. No, it's not giving something up—it's exchanging, selling," I said. "Just like how we rented this hotel room for one night. Tomorrow at noon, this comfort will disappear. The supply gets cut off because we can only afford to buy it for a limited time. That's why we need money. Without money, we can't buy anything."

Hei Jian didn't respond. He seemed to have drifted off to sleep. I examined him closely and discovered that the handsome face that he had always meticulously taken care of was marred by tiny wrinkles and crow's feet.

I pondered my dad's life. He began working in a factory when he was still in high school. His grades were less than stellar, but he was very smart and super passionate about moviemaking. Eventually, he summoned enough courage to apply for the film school of his dreams as a young-worker applicant, and he actually got in. But his good fortune was short-lived. He was like a nugget of gold buried in the sand. He attracted the loving attention of many young women, including Jie. She was his first girlfriend.

When Jie became pregnant with his child soon after they had started going out, she didn't want to get an abortion. She even wrote a letter to his program, informing them of her situation. She wanted him to marry her so they could live together, happily ever after. But she was sorely disappointed. Instead of marrying her, Hei Jian suddenly saw her as his enemy. She realized that her dream of happiness was destined for doom. Soon after, she left the baby with him and walked out. And from that moment on, his life of hell and misery truly began.

Was Hei Jian at fault for what he did? Was he right or wrong in his choices? All I knew was that I felt infinitely grateful for him. I was thankful that he hadn't just abandoned me or pawned me off to somebody else. He could totally have chosen to do that. He could have just minded his own business and continued to pursue his dream career.

But he didn't. Instead, he picked me up and carried me on his back and marched on. Without me around, he would probably have gone on to live a much easier and prosperous life. Maybe he'd have graduated from that film school, and his prospects would have been vastly different.

What was he to do now? He had no inheritance, no steady income, a foul temper, and a child to take care of. Suddenly, I realized that I've always complained about him trying to date women while refusing to give me a mom. But perhaps I was wrong about him. Perhaps the issue wasn't that he couldn't make long-term commitments. Perhaps it was the other people in his life who, whenever things became tough or complicated, would back out. Perhaps he was just a sad loser who, out of excessive pride, had pretended to be someone he wasn't.

≋ Chapter 10

My First Day Back to School was Foggy and Dreary

My first day back to school from winter break was a foggy, dreary day. But it didn't put me in a bad mood. I had succeeded in collecting my school fees for the semester from two sources that weren't Hei Jian. Yesterday in the hotel, while I was staring at Hei Jian's sleeping face, I'd had another epiphany that would quietly transform my life. I'd decided that I wasn't going to ask Hei Jian for any more money. The responsibility of caring for me was choking the life out of him. I didn't want to pull him down anymore. I wanted to share his load.

Jie was my first target. I told her I was about to drop out of school because Hei Jian didn't have enough money to pay my registration fees.

She was livid. "What, are you telling me that an able-bodied, grown man like him can't even afford to take care of a school-aged child?"

"But he's already put me through school for five years. And you haven't," I replied coldly.

"What, did he teach you to keep saying something like that? You go tell him. Even for married couples, it's the man's job to be the bread-winner of the family. If he can't do that, why call himself a man?"

I didn't want to hear her keep saying those things, so I interrupted her: "Today is the final deadline to pay my school fees."

"I thought he would be all rich and famous by now. A bigshot celebrity of some kind. Turns out he's not that impressive after all." She asked me for Hei Jian's cell number. I said I didn't know because he kept changing numbers and I hadn't had the chance to memorize his newest.

Jie couldn't do anything more about it, so she stared at me, seething. I stared back at her, defiant. I had the right to look at her that way. I knew what my classmates' moms did for them. What had she done for me? Sure, our circumstances were a bit unique, but was it my fault?

She paced back and forth in the room. She made many calls. Some of those calls made her really upset, because as soon as she hung up, she started to cuss the other person out using a string of rather nasty words. She kept calling and calling, until it was almost noontime. Then she said she had to go out to get the money for my school. It was nearly evening when she returned. Looking irritated, she handed an envelope to me. It contained my registration fees.

"I don't have that much money on hand. I had to borrow it from someone else." Her voice was cheerless.

"You know, if I were you guys, I wouldn't have chosen to give birth to a baby," I said. "And even if somehow the baby ended up being born, I would have strangled him to death before he came of age. Much better that than letting him die hungry and destitute later on." I took the money without thanking her; I just left her with those words.

"Come back here, you heartless boy!" she shouted after me. "Get back here!!"

I ignored her. Hugging the envelope, I dashed away.

After leaving Jie's place, I went to see my aunt—my grandma's niece, the one that took possession of Nainai's house. I gave her the same talk: it was the last day to pay the fees to my school, but I still couldn't get ahold of Hei Jian. My aunt did seem to have some tender feelings left for me. My nainai had told me that when I was a baby, my aunt had helped her take care of me for a while. Apparently, my aunt had even considered adopting me. But Hei Jian had shut her down pretty quickly.

When my aunt greeted me at the door, she acted very warm and enthusiastic. But as soon as I told her about the problem with my school fees, her enthusiasm cooled rapidly.

"Did Hei Jian send you here?" she asked.

"Nope. I haven't seen him in over six months," I lied. "I don't even know where he is."

"Poor child. Look how thin you are! You look like a little starving monkey. What have you been eating?" She avoided the topic of my school fees, but she did bring me some food and snacks.

I looked around this once-familiar place. I had lived here for years until Nainai passed away. But the furniture had been rearranged since then. It looked different now.

"What are you looking for?" asked my aunt.

"I'm trying to find Nainai's picture. It used to hang up there. And there was a photo of me and Hei Jian right next to it." I pointed to a spot on the wall.

I saw my aunt avert her gaze. I kept talking. "I often dream about Nainai. Lately, Nainai has been telling me that I can't rely on my dad anymore, and that I should come to you for help instead."

Her eyes widened. "Did your nainai really say that?"

"Yeah. Just last night, she told me, 'Go see your aunt. She bought a tortoise fish and will surely offer you a bowl of fish soup.'" I saw a thin film of water misting her eyes. What had actually happened was that I snuck by her place yesterday morning and saw her returning from the farmer's market, tortoise fish dangling from her hand.

My aunt handed me the money without issue, but she gave one condition. She asked me not to visit her on weekends, because that's when the rest of her family—her son, her daughter, and her grandchildren—would all be home. When my aunt inherited Nainai's estate, Hei Jian got into a bunch of massive arguments with her and her family, after which they were completely estranged.

So, that's how I came up with twice the amount of money I needed for school. Carrying the bills, I entered the basement room of an apartment building. The room belonged to one of Hei Jian's buddies and

Hei Jian was temporarily living there. He had lost his latest girlfriend and now he had lost his job again. In the past, he could always cozy up to Jing and stay with her, but that was no longer an option. That night when he stormed out of her place and took me with him to live in a hotel, he had burned all his bridges. And now he was hiding out in a basement room, sleeping soundly all day with the excuse that he needed to regroup and plan out his next steps. But the basement was too musty. After sleeping there for only two days, Hei Jian had begun to feel unwell. He developed a hacking cough and diarrhea, but he stubbornly refused to go to the hospital. He just kept slumbering away, because according to him, "sleep is the best medicine for all ailments."

I handed him half of the money I collected and told him to go get checked by a doctor. The rest of the money I was going to take to school later that day. Hei Jian didn't question me on where all that money came from. He simply said, "Good job. Well deserved."

Before I headed out to school to get registered, he called me to his bedside and grabbed me by my hand. He pulled me in for a hug.

"My boy, trust me, our good days are coming. And when they come, they will sweep us up like the surging tides of the ocean—like a tsunami! It will be magnificent . . . unstoppable." Hei Jian's eyes glinted. "Oh, I forgot to tell you. I recently got introduced to someone, a big fish in the movie industry. I'm just trying to think about how I can best collaborate with him. See? Good fortune is already beckoning us."

In the afternoon, after completing my school registration, I returned to the basement of the building to see if Hei Jian was feeling better. The door was locked. There was nobody inside the room. I wandered around the place until I discovered a small scrap of paper stuck to the bottom corner of the door. It was a note from Hei Jian.

*Dear son,*

*I'm leaving here. Just remember this: no matter what happens, don't lose hope, and never give up. You must keep going. We must keep going.*

*Dad*

He didn't even bother writing out our names. Maybe it was intentional. Maybe he didn't want anybody else to read the note.

I felt like an idiot. Why did I give him all that money? Twelve hundred yuan was no small sum—it was more than enough to buy him a train ticket out of town. But then again, what other choice was there? If I hadn't given him the money, he would have been trapped inside this dank, moldy basement.

On the flipside, he probably would have found a way to get out of here eventually. It's kind of bizarre, but Hei Jian has this uncanny ability to escape from the most difficult situations, even when trapped at the bottom of a pit.

After I found out Hei Jian had left, I suddenly felt very sad and down. I slowly inched my way back toward school, wondering when we would be able to see each other again. Suddenly, I saw Jie. She was walking with Uncle Li. They both looked kind of upset. He walked ahead while she treaded closely behind. Every few steps, Uncle Li would stop to say something to her, then he would resume walking. With her head held high, Jie looked like she was indifferent to whatever he was saying. Finally, she said something which seemed to completely infuriate him. He raised his fist at her. Concealed by the row of trees lining the street, I followed them stealthily, drawing closer until I was able to hear their conversation.

"No. It's not about the money. Money is the minor concern. It's a matter of principle. That's the bigger issue here. If he was able to coax money out of you today, he will try to get more money from you tomorrow. And the next day, and the day after that . . . Who knows what reason he will come up with next time? I have to be blunt in saying this, but it's like feeding a bottomless well. If you're smart enough, you'd wash your hands of it now!"

"Damn your principles!" Jie retorted. "When you went back to your hometown and saw all those nieces and nephews of yours, you gifted them each five hundred to eight hundred yuan! Did I say a word about it?!" I could see her face burning with fury.

"But those are my relatives. Of course I have to be nice to them."

"Relatives? Bai Jian is my son!"

"Are you still holding on to that? Do you really believe he'll come around, start seeing you as his mom? Don't be foolish! You have been strangers, and you will *stay* strangers! Maybe worse. Maybe you can't even be strangers . . . because he hates you! Everybody tells him to hate you. They've been telling him that since he was a baby."

"I don't care. He's my flesh and blood. A piece of me. Even if he hates me, he is still my son. And nobody can deny that. Even if he doesn't treat me as his mom, I'm still his mother."

"In that case, why did you abandon him?"

"It's none of your fucking business!"

Strutting with proud defiance, she quickened her steps and overtook Uncle Li in a matter of seconds. I crouched down, picked up a small pebble, and threw it at him. But that rock was way too light and way too small. It landed quietly on the ground, closer to me than to him.

Strange. Even though Jie fought for me, I didn't feel much sympathy toward her. Nor did I feel any guilt or regret.

I felt nothing.

## 🌧️ Chapter 11

It Rained for an Entire Week

It rained for an entire week. Everybody cursed the terrible weather, but I was secretly delighted—one of my classmates had told me that if the rain didn't stop falling by Friday, he wouldn't go home for the weekend because his parents would have to make a trip to the countryside to purchase some type of goods. He wasn't quite sure what kind of product it was. All he knew was that his parents owned a business, and they lived in a large condo that measured over two hundred square meters smack in the middle of the city. Although his place was not that far from our school, he was too chicken to stay home alone. I looked down on him for that. If it was me—even if I owned no big house, even if I owned just two square meters of space—I would be rolling around on the floor, cackling with joy. And I would be more than happy to stay home by myself. But despite my scorn for him, I was still secretly glad to have someone stay with me at school for the weekend. At the end of the day, it was better to have a pigeon-hearted guy as company than to stay in an empty dorm all by myself.

Hei Jian had said to me at the hotel after the New Year, "Son, you've grown up. You are a young man now. When the weekends come around, why don't you stay in the school dorm and pretend like it's just another weekday? It's pretty simple: you sleep, then you wake up. And when you're sleeping, you won't even notice a difference. No matter where you go to sleep, it's pretty much the same." He continued, "We don't need to beg anybody for favors. We've had our challenges and difficulties in the past. But now that it's a brand new year and we're not the same old Hei Jian and Bai Jian anymore, nothing can stand in our way."

What could I say to that? I had to keep going and try my best to be brave. Luckily for me, I would have some company that first week of the semester. The rain was like God's special blessing—a gift for me and me alone. But by noon, it had changed. The rain stopped falling, and the sky brightened. All the wet puddles and patches on the road began to dry up. By the end of the second period in the afternoon, I was dismayed to see that the sun which had been hiding behind soggy grey clouds for an entire week had re-emerged. My companion immediately ran toward my seat and danced and shouted with glee, "Look, Bai Jian! The rain has stopped. My parents are coming to pick me up. I can go home now!"

I rolled my eyes at him, then stared up at the sky.

When the last period of the day came around, I told myself not to look outside anymore. As always, there was a swarm of parents waiting to pick up their kids. They glued their faces to the windows and peered into our classroom. After all the other students had left, I got up from my desk.

On Friday evenings, the school cafeteria didn't supply any dinner. I planned to go out to buy some food and bring it back to my dorm room to eat. I figured having something to chew on might help me shake off some of that fear and anxiety.

But when I exited into the hallway, I saw Jing. She was standing there, still as a statue.

"I've been watching you, Bai Jian. You didn't look too keen for your classes to end."

Jing was wearing a white shirt. Looks like she was truly ready to say goodbye to the color blue forever. She asked me to come along with her to do some shopping at a nearby supermarket. Then we would head back to her little apartment.

"Hei Jian must have told you not to come to my place on the weekends anymore, right?" she asked.

I nodded. I couldn't lie to her. I'm okay deceiving some people—I can lie to them without even batting an eye—but for others, I simply can't bring myself to do it.

Jing let me pick out my favorite snacks at the supermarket. I looked up and down and all around, then grabbed a few packs of instant noodles with different flavors.

She tossed them back on the racks and fumed, "Why instant noodles? Are they the only thing you know how to eat? Look here!" She looked pissed off as she grabbed a whole bunch of brightly packaged products off the shelf and dumped them into our cart. She was moving so fast, I could barely catch what she was doing. I think she got chocolate, yogurt drink, sweet bread, sponge cake, pistachios, walnuts, jelly cups, seaweed snacks, chewing gum, and some fruit.

When we left the supermarket, Jing suddenly looked very happy. "Hey Bai Jian, do you know what special day today is?"

I looked at her, confused.

"Today's the day I decided to prepare myself for marriage."

I snickered. "Oh, you're only getting ready to be married . . . not *actually* getting married. Is that worth being so excited?"

"Of course. For me, this is a significant life decision." She glanced at me and asked, "Aren't you curious who I'm preparing to marry?"

"Must be that Brother Quan," I said.

"No. It's someone you have never met before. Actually, nobody in my life knows him. I met him just last week."

"Last week? And when do you plan on getting married?"

"Next week."

"Gosh! Are you guys, like, love at first sight or something?"

"Ha, so you know about love at first sight too?" Jing was beaming. This was highly unusual. She rarely expressed so much with her face. She usually looked calm and composed.

"So, who is the man anyways?"

"After we get home, I'll show you his picture." She continued to smile.

When we got home, Jing began cooking dinner for us. She cleaned up her little table so that I could do my homework. She seemed to have completely forgotten about the photo. When we had finished eating, I reminded her, "You were going to show me that person's picture?" She turned around to look for it. I secretly prayed in my heart that she would take out Hei Jian's picture. Although I knew it was impossible, I really wanted that to happen. Perhaps I was becoming a bit delusional?

I'm not sure how I felt when I first saw the picture. It was the photo of a blind person. His features weren't particularly handsome. He didn't look that young either.

Actually, it wasn't really a photo. It was a newspaper clipping containing an article written about him.

Jing seemed not to mind that he was blind. When she talked about him, her eyes lit up, and her facial features would shift away from their normal, restrained positions.

"Did you know? Not only is he an excellent massage therapist, he's also a very accomplished Chinese traditional medicine doctor. With a touch of his hand, he can instantly tell how healthy a person is. He can figure out what diseases they have and how severe, and how much longer they have to live. His diagnostic skills are more accurate and reliable than any medical device."

She carefully stored away that page of newspaper and continued to tell me about him.

"After I read about him in that journal article, I went to find him. At that time, I wasn't in a good place physically or emotionally. But no need to go into the details. In short, I'm just so glad that I met him that day. He truly stunned me and shook my world. I had never felt that way about anyone before. When I found out that he's not in a marital relationship, I introduced myself to him. I shared with him about my work, my background, my family . . . After he heard me out, he was silent for a while. Then he said, 'Before I can make a decision, I must feel your face.' So I drew close to him and put my face right up against his. After some time, he said, 'Okay.'

"When I asked him about it later—why he wanted to put our faces together to decide—he told me that his hands are in constant contact with people's bodies due to his line of work. He worried that his ability to receive and interpret emotional signals using hands have been affected by the chaotic emotions that his clients carry with them every day. That's why he chose to use his face instead."

I couldn't help reminding her that he was blind.

"Why does that matter? When we get together, it's like . . . like a tree sitting with a flower. We respect each other, and we lean on each other for support. Isn't that enough?"

"But . . ." I still felt that something was off. But I couldn't put my thoughts into words.

"I know what you're trying to say. You are worried about me. You're such a kind boy, Bai Jian. But lately, my views on a lot of things have completely changed. For instance, I realized that what I want in life is not a romantic lover but a compatible partner to temper my anxiety, fear, and loneliness. Someone who would bring peace into my heart and inspire me to become a better person. These are not the kind of things Hei Jian can offer me. Aside from some sparks of passion and a fleeting illusion, his presence only brings me distress and despair. I think he's more suited to being a woman's first love. And in the end, very few women marry their first love."

Honestly, my interest was waning. Plus I couldn't really understand all the stuff that she was saying. The only thing I understood was that Hei Jian was getting kicked out of her life. Permanently.

"Bai Jian, please be happy for me. It's a dream come true for me to marry this person. He will be my gentle giant, my rock and pillar— always there to comfort me and give me strength. Not weigh me down like Hei Jian."

Then she rambled on about him a little more. "He'd always make me feel so anxious and on edge. He's like a wild, roaring stream, or a fidgety arm that would jump and spasm at any moment—so dangerous and unpredictable! Actually, could we stay on the topic of Hei Jian a little longer? Because after today, I'm going to erase his name from my mind." She kept going. "Where is Hei Jian now? What's he doing? Will he marry Wei? Where will they live? Are they going to have their own baby? Will he be a good dad to the child?"

Just when I was about to reply *I don't know* to all those questions, I realized that she was not expecting a response from me. Jing was staring blankly into a patch of empty space in front of her as she asked her endless string of questions. It was like she was talking and venting to an invisible person standing there.

"What is love? I think I've finally grasped it. Love is an illusion you weave. And when you *do* fall in love, what you have fallen in love with is not a person, but rather, the feelings—the illusion of happiness that the person gives you."

I think I understood her point a little bit now. Hei Jian often gave me illusions too. For example, when he would watch soccer on TV, he would make me believe that he was the number one soccer coach in the world. He would yell, "Dumbass! Get your act together! Sub that player already! Get so-and-so off the field and put so-and-so on!" And more often than not, the coach of that team really did substitute the players like he said.

Another example was that when Hei Jian watched movies, he would talk nonstop. "Zoom in a bit. Pan this way. Pan that way. Again. Take a long shot. Now hold steady . . . Good! What the hell? Why are you shaking your camera so much? Are you scared people won't get what you're trying to say? Idiot!" During those moments, he gave me the illusion that he was a big shot director.

When Hei Jian was in a happy mood, he liked to recite long paragraphs of movie script. One instant he would be one character, and a different one the next. He would shift his tone of voice frequently; even his facial expressions changed dramatically from moment to moment. So much so, it would send shivers down my spine. I would gaze at him in total admiration, convinced that he was some famous movie star. But in truth, and in reality, Hei Jian is none of those things. He's just an ordinary guy who rotates through jobs and who's always strapped for cash.

After the weekend was over, and before I went back to school, Jing told me that it was the last time I'd see her in this little apartment. Starting the following week, she was moving to a new home. Her husband-to-be had recently purchased a spacious apartment for them, in a prime spot downtown. Of course, if I wanted to, I could still visit her at her new home. But I would need to assume a new identity in front of the blind doctor, she said. I would no longer be Hei Jian's son Bai Jian, but a distant nephew of Jing's. Someone whom Jing had been asked to look after on weekends.

I agreed to this arrangement on the surface, but I knew that I wouldn't be going to Jing's new place. Despite my hopes and my eagerness to become part of her new life, I was just an accessory, a dependent of Hei Jian. If he was getting cancelled from her life, my existence was going to become meaningless to her too.

## Chapter 12

Spring Brought along Annoying Plane Tree Catkins

With the arrival of spring came its flying army of catkins. Thanks to a horde of London plane trees growing in the school yard just outside our window, the fuzzy, prickly balls rolled off branches, bouncing and swirling through the air like a bunch of naughty sprites. The catkins snuck in through the open window of the classroom and swarmed us, making my head drowsy and my nose runny and me itch all over.

One day, I just couldn't take it anymore. I requested a day of absence from class, and laid down in my cool, quiet dorm room. I felt much better instantly.

Upon discovering this secret solution, I no longer wanted to go back to sitting inside my over-ventilated classroom. I began to find all sorts of reasons and excuses to stay in the dorm—or simply skipped my classes. I decided to self-study all the materials in the comfort of my room.

The head teacher eventually found me out. She didn't think that I could learn everything on my own. She also refused to believe that my seasonal allergies were so bad they could actually prevent me from attending class. She insisted that I was hiding in the dorm and planning some kind of mischief, although she had no clue what I was actually up to.

She started forcing me back to class every time I was absent. But I would just skip out again when nobody was paying attention. Little by little, I came to enjoy this game of hide and seek. I wondered if they would still be able to find me if I crawled under the bed instead of lying on top of it? Just when I was about to test out my plan, I found the metal gate at the entrance of the dorm building padlocked. I knew it was designed to keep me out, because this gate was never locked up before I started to regularly skip classes.

Eventually, I came up with another creative solution: I stayed in class but wore a face mask inside the classroom. Somehow, that too offended the dignity of my teachers. At the beginning of each class, they would quietly stare at me with an icy gaze until I removed my mask. Only then would they start to teach the lesson for the day.

One day, during my Chinese literature class, a little yellow butterfly fluttered in through the window and circled the head of the person sitting right in front of me. Despite my efforts, I just couldn't stop myself from staring at it.

My teacher called out my name and taunted, "Even if you're destined to become a rich and famous celebrity someday, Bai Jian, you should still make an effort to learn this material. It will only benefit you, not harm."

Later that day, Hei Jian swept into my school like a gust of wind. The first thing he did was to blare out to the entire world that he was working nearby, helping to reshoot some scenes for a big-budget movie. Apparently he had networked his way up to that big fish director, and even got a nice new job out of it. His self-esteem ballooned. "Hey, kid, y'know, your dad is a real movie person now!"

Actually, from the moment he walked in, I had sensed that something was up. It was like he was high on drugs or something. His eyes burned with an unnatural brightness. He was so restless, he couldn't sit or stand still. He swayed his body this way and that, shifting his pose constantly. And every so often, he grabbed me by the shoulder and shook me vigorously. "Hey, kid, you really are doing great here. You face is chubby. Your body has really filled out."

Hei Jian had acquired this weird new accent and changed his way of speaking. Instead of saying "we," he now said "us guys." Instead of saying "do this" or "do that," he would say "fix this" or "fix that." Also, he kept inserting foreign words like "OK" randomly into his sentences. I really regret taking him to see my teachers. Even though he commanded me to do it, I could have just lied and told him that my teachers were in the middle of giving a lesson or that they had gone out to run some errands.

When Hei Jian first stepped inside the teachers' office, he cleared his throat, as if to declare his arrival. Then he yelled, "Hey everybody!"

A couple of teachers turned around and glanced at him. One of them asked coolly, "Who are you looking for?"

Fortunately, my head teacher recognized him. "Bai Jian's dad, right?"

He was eventually given a seat. He shoved his sunglasses high up on his head, dangled one foot off the ground, and began to ramble on and on. "I can collaborate with your school. Get you set up with an acting class, or an acting camp for the summer. The top performing students will get the golden ticket opportunity to be recommended to one of those film schools backed by the big shots in the movie industry. There, they'll have loads of opportunities to make it big. Ordinary folks may think that the entertainment industry is very mysterious and out of reach. But I tell ya, it just takes that one right connection to get you in the door. And once your foot is in the door, you're all set. It's only a matter of time before you become rich and famous."

"Maybe you should turn your own son into a celebrity first," one teacher smirked. "Then our school will become known as the 'home school of the movie star' and we teachers will get a little extra boost of fame too."

"Well, Bai Jian's not like me." Hei Jian waved his hand dismissively. "He's got no raw acting talent. You need talent to go into certain fields."

"You haven't been around to teach him or guide him and you blame it on the lack of talent?" my head teacher interjected.

"Look at the other parents. They stay with their kids every day. Even if one of them isn't available, the other one will pick up the slack and spend more time with their child. As for you, you're like a guest visitor. Dropping in to see your son briefly once or twice a year."

My head teacher went on to suggest that Hei Jian should dedicate more time and energy to me, because, "Children grow up so fast, and once that window of opportunity passes, it will be very difficult to catch up later on. Of course we teachers do our best to help, but we cannot replace a child's parents."

Hei Jian never enjoyed receiving criticism—he didn't take to my teachers' words kindly. His face turned dark and gloomy as he demanded, "Is something going on with Bai Jian? From the sounds of what you're telling me, he's a problem child." Then he turned to face me. "What kind of trouble have you gotten into?"

"A student shouldn't need to be in trouble to catch our attention," the head teacher responded. "Education is all about prevention and protection against that possibility."

"Oh, you got me worried for a second. I thought something was wrong. Well, our country's education system is all messed up. Just take a look at the students from some of the other countries! When they graduate from their school system, every one of them is independent and confident. As for our kids, even if they start out with unique personalities and talents, they all get ironed out by our schools and turned into identical copies of each other."

"You don't need to lecture us about it. If you have questions or concerns, you should write to the Ministry of Education, or you can send your child to a foreign country to study."

It was excruciatingly painful for me to listen to that conversation. But Hei Jian was completely oblivious.

"I don't really care about his grades—I just care about whether or not he's happy. If he's got perfect marks on all his subjects, but feels sad and miserable every day, then I don't want him to have those perfect marks."

"But how do you know whether or not he is happy?" another teacher chirped. "*We* don't know." I saw the corner of the head teacher's lips curl up before she exited the office. Soon, one of the other teachers left too. Eventually, they all left.

I lifted my head and stared at Hei Jian angrily. "Don't come here anymore in the future. Whenever you're here, you screw everything up for me."

Hei Jian looked back at me, speechless. After some time, he took out a pack of cigarettes and started to smoke.

After a while the school janitor came over and glared at Hei Jian, pointing to the "No Smoking" sign on the wall. "Didn't you see that? Smoking's not allowed around here!"

For a moment, Hei Jian looked dazed. Then he hurled the cigarette butt on the floor, got up, and left.

I bent down, picked up the cigarette butt, and tossed it into the garbage bin.

"Why, the son is more mature than the dad . . ." mumbled the janitor.

I joined Hei Jian on the curb outside the school. "You really don't need to come here anymore," I said, softer now. "You even said it before—I've already grown up. I can stay at school alone on the weekends."

"Why don't you go to Jie's place? You have every right to visit her."

"I just want to stay at school by myself. I want to learn to be more independent!" What I actually wanted to say was that I didn't want Jie and Uncle Li to fight over me again. When someone becomes the reason that other people argue, that means his existence is a headache to them—an annoyance. I didn't want to be annoying to anyone.

"What about Jing's place?" he asked.

"Seems like, to you, there are a lot of places I can go."

"So why don't you go there?"

I glared at him now.

"I know Jing likes you. Even if she doesn't like me anymore, she will never not like you. I'm sure of it."

"I don't want to exploit other people's goodwill."

Hei Jian's eyes opened wide. "What do you mean by that?"

So I told him the truth. "Jing just moved away. If I visit her at her new place, I'll have to tell everyone that I'm her nephew. I don't want to accidentally say the wrong things and cause trouble for her. Oh, by the way, she's getting married."

"Have you met her husband? What does he look like?"

I was quiet for a long time before responding. "He's a blind man. He was born that way. She seems very happy to be with him. She calls him her gentle giant."

"Really?!" Hei Jian seemed shocked. He stared at me with gaping eyes, as if I had the most unbelievable piece of news printed all over my face. After a long pause, he murmured, "Holy shit!" But just then, his phone rang. As he took the call, he bolted up, lumped a pleasant smile on his face, and stooped his body, like he was bowing toward someone big and important standing right in front of him.

"Yes, yes, I'm heading out right away. I'll get those photocopies for you by tonight at the latest. Yes, I know, I won't disappoint you. No, no, no, I don't need to visit him at his school. He's doing fantastic there. My presence will only be a distraction to him. Yeah, it's just like what you said, 'A man must take care of his career first.'"

After hanging up, Hei Jian said, "It's him, the big wig I told you about. He doesn't know I'm here." He wrapped me inside a burly hug. "Son, I have to go now." He strode off, then spun around and looked me in the eye. "Are you sure you don't want me to come here anymore?"

I turned my head away and refused to answer.

Now he had even more excuses not to visit me. Apparently, this new boss of his didn't want him to see me or get involved in any relationships. And Hei Jian seemed to absolutely worship him. He was convinced he would be able to achieve great things under this boss. But from my perspective, I was feeling less and less confident about his chances of success. A person destined for great things should not be dangling his feet and blabbering on noisily in front of his son's teachers. He shouldn't be gloating shamelessly, trying to offend all the educators at school.

Maybe his boss really was some big wig. Because a few days later, I came across this splashy article in the local newspaper talking about the film crew. It was a big deal: not that many film crews visited our boring little town. The article was very long, very enthusiastic, and very detailed. It gave full descriptions and listings of all the personnel working on set, including all the assistants to Mr. Big Wig Director. I searched through that article line by line, trying to find Hei Jian's name, but there was no mention of him anywhere inside. Right then, a thought came to me: the call that Hei Jian had answered the other day probably hadn't come directly from Mr. Big Wig himself. It was from one of his assistants, maybe, or an assistant to an assistant of his assistant.

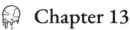 **Chapter 13**

The Consequences of Global Warming

Because of global warming, the summers in our city have become hotter and hotter. There was no air conditioning inside my classroom and no electric fans either. All forty of us were squashed together inside the melting pot, drowning in the sour stench of our sweaty B.O.

Things were even worse inside our dorm. In addition to the torturous heat, there were also mosquitoes. And some idiot always forgot to shut the window screen, or just left the screen open on purpose. Those pesky mosquitoes had all developed resistance to the mosquito repellents we used. Even when we lit up two coils of mosquito incense at the same time, they still managed to get to us. Good sleep was becoming harder and harder to come by—I would toss and turn for quite a while before drifting off. Even after I had finally fallen asleep, the buzzing of mosquitoes would soon wake me up again. One night, I was unable to fall asleep at all, so I had to lie in bed with my eyes open the entire night.

I craved a wholesome night's sleep, and I was determined to make my wish a reality.

I pretended to pay attention in class, but inside my head, I secretly analyzed a list of names and faces, trying to decide the best target for my mission. In the end, I chose my old aunt. I decided to invite myself to her place for a sleepover. The last time I saw her, she had told me not to visit her on weekends because the rest of her family would all be there. To avoid stirring up any trouble, I decided to visit her on a Wednesday. I think I had the right to sleep over there for at least one night. Sure, my aunt had inherited Nainai's house and made herself the legal owner of the place, but . . . I missed my nainai. Why couldn't I go over to pay my respects and take a good look at Nainai's picture?

"It's really you?" My aunt was quite surprised to see me. "What are you doing here?"

I told her the truth, and she didn't say no to me. All she said was, "Alright, I will let things go this time. But next time, if you decide to come over, make sure you give me call me ahead of time. Okay?" She sent me to sleep in her bedroom. I sat down on the edge of the bed, and before I even took off my backpack, I was overtaken by drowsy sleep.

When I woke up, I found myself on the floor of the storage room. An old straw mat was spread out under my body. A new rash had appeared on my arm. It was a large, red, angry-looking patch; my skin burned with pain. This was either the dirty work of a poisonous ant or the mark of a spider who decided to take a stroll on my body. I knew this because I'd experienced it in the past.

Hunger pangs attacked my belly and I realized that my aunt hadn't woken me up to eat dinner. Perhaps I had fallen so deep in my slumber that even when she moved me from her bedroom to the storage room, I didn't wake up. In that case, I definitely wouldn't have woken up if someone had just called my name a couple of times.

My aunt was not home. There was no one else around either. Perhaps she'd gone out to the farmer's market to buy some vegetables? I knew it was part of her daily routine to visit the farmer's market early in the morning. I went into the kitchen to look for something to eat. Other than a jar of pickled vegetables, there was nothing in sight. And those pickled vegetables looked ancient. I fished out a piece of pickled cowpea and managed to take one single bite before spitting it out. Its sour taste stung my eyes and made me tear up instantly.

I opened up the kitchen drawers one by one. Still, nothing to eat at all, only some dried noodles. But not instant noodles—these had to be cooked in a pot. Buried deep inside one of the drawers was a little rusted metal box. It looked like a cookie tin. I shook it. Something was in there. When I opened it, there were no cookies inside, just several small bundles of rolled-up cash. I was about to close the lid and put the tin back in place, but I hesitated. Maybe I could use one of those bills to buy myself some breakfast. If I only took one, she shouldn't notice. I stuck two fingers into one of the rolls and drew out a bill. It wasn't a small bill; actually, it was one of the largest. I folded it up and quickly shoved it into my pant pocket. I had to rush. I must leave here before my aunt got back. But when I reached the door, I felt an invisible force pulling down on my legs.

What if I took two bills—one for this morning's breakfast and one for the dinner I missed last night? And since my aunt allowed the bugs in her storage room to bite me, she should at least foot the cost of my medical treatment, right? And before that, she and her family had plotted together to steal this house from me and Hei Jian. "Conspiracy," "larceny," "robbery," and "invasion"—those were the words Hei Jian had hurled at them when they had those big arguments. A house is worth a lot of money. Although my aunt had lent me some money for school, that amount was puny compared to what she had previously taken from us. When I realized this, I returned to the kitchen, opened up the box and removed all the large bills. Before I left, I stopped again. Since I was already going to expose myself, why not just take the whole tin with me? The old box was destined for some garbage bin anyway. And if I insisted that I'd never gone into her kitchen—even if she was suspicious of me—she wouldn't be able to do anything about it.

On my way back to school, I saw my old aunt walking with a basket full of vegetables on her arm. But she didn't see me. Her body posture looked tense—she rushed along with small, shuffling steps. I hid behind a tree bush and pondered, How would she react when she discovered that her treasure box was missing?

I started to feel even more nervous and uneasy. I didn't use the money to buy breakfast; instead, I hurried back to school. Funnily enough, my belly no longer growled with hunger.

My aunt found out quicker than I expected. When we were eating lunch in the school's cafeteria, she stormed in. "Bai Jian, did you take that metal box from my kitchen?"

*Whoosh.* Every set of eyes in the cafeteria turned to focus on my face.

"What metal box? I didn't take anything. And anyway, why would I take something like that?" My body started to tremble, but I kept on pretending like there was nothing wrong.

"Don't lie! It must have been you," she hissed. "Before I went out to the farmer's market this morning, I took some cash out of the box. And by the time I returned, the whole thing was gone! There was no one else in the house except you. So, if it wasn't you, who else could it be?" She spoke faster and faster. Her chubby cheeks turned redder and more flushed.

"But I never went into your kitchen!" I retorted loudly. I must stay strong, or all was lost.

"What do you mean you haven't been into the kitchen? On the counter there's an opened jar of pickle beans with the juices spilled everywhere! You left the lid off. Who are you trying to deceive?"

Oh shit. That was so stupid of me. I had totally forgotten about it.

"Give it back now! Otherwise, I'm taking you to the police station."

I slumped my shoulders as I stood before her, staring at her feet, unable to find the words to defend myself.

One of the girls fetched my backpack from the classroom and handed it to my aunt. She grabbed it and ripped open the zipper. She only had to take one look inside to discover the metal box. "And you told me you didn't take it? What's this then? I never realized that you were a three-handed thief."

She opened the box right in front of everybody and began to count its contents. Perhaps because there was no money missing, she said nothing more. She threw my backpack on the floor, hugged her metal box to herself, and headed out. But before she reached the door, she turned around and said stiffly, "Don't come back anymore. If you come, I won't open the door."

"I'm not a thief, YOU are a thief!" I hollered. "No . . . you're a robber! You stole our house. You made us homeless. I'll never forget what you did to us, for as long as I live!" I was screaming by the end.

My old aunt stayed where she was, as if planning to debate me. But then she checked herself. She turned her round body on its heel and quickly shuffled off.

I snatched up the steel food tray in front of me and dashed toward the garbage bin. I dumped my nearly untouched lunch—stir-fried shredded potato, tomato and egg soup, soy stewed eggplant, and a small chunk of dry, hard rice—all into the garbage. Then I tossed the tray into a different bin.

I felt dizzy and faint. I stepped outside. The blazing sun beat down on me, making me feel even more woozy. I headed toward a classroom but the door to the room was locked. I had nowhere else to go, so I slowly walked back to the dorm.

I could hear that the dorm room was bustling with noise and commotion. All the kids in there were trying to speak at the same time.

"I don't want to live in the same room as a thief. I want to switch rooms."

"Last week, I lost five yuan. Maybe he stole it."

"No wonder he kept skipping class and locking himself inside our dorm. He was probably plotting these devious things."

"Did you see his hands? His fingers are so long and flexible. That's what the hands of a thief look like."

I stood outside the door, unsure whether or not to enter. In the end, I decided to go in. If I didn't enter now, it would be even harder to go in later. But as soon as I stepped in, the room fell silent. It was as if an ice cube had just been dropped into a boiling pot—everything cooled down instantly.

"I'm NOT a thief," I announced. "I was only trying to get back what was rightfully mine! She was the one who invaded our family home and drove me and my dad into the streets."

I don't know whether or not they believed me. But they all stared at me, and no one said a thing. So I climbed into bed, grabbed my blanket, and pulled it over my head.

In the afternoon, the atmosphere in our classroom felt kind of weird. My desk mate was nowhere to be found, and his desk drawer had been completely emptied. I tried to reassure myself that this was actually a blessing in disguise, because I finally had the entire desk to myself.

The following morning, my head teacher sought me out and asked me for Hei Jian's phone number, saying that she needed to speak with him about something. I gave her a number. She came back a few minutes later. "That number is no longer in service. Give me his newest number."

"But that's the only number I have."

My teacher didn't seem to believe me. "Are you afraid to talk to him? Or do you just not want me to talk with him? It's useless though, you can't dodge it forever."

Later that day, I read through all the local newspapers. I finally found one article about the movie crew. They had already left. Which meant Hei Jian left town without saying goodbye. He was either too busy, or he had taken Mr. Big Wig's advice to heart.

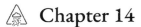 **Chapter 14**

The Wedding Motorcade Paraded through
Rain-Soaked Streets

The wedding motorcade paraded through rain-soaked streets. There were a total of eleven cars in the fleet. Jing said that the number eleven signifies "being together with one heart and one mind." The entire wedding fleet was wrapped with garlands of fresh, blooming flowers and layers of colorful balloons.

The car leading the procession was adorned with a pair of custom-made miniature figurines on its hood. The figurines were about one foot high and made to look like the bride and groom.

Jing was dressed in an off-the-shoulder white wedding gown. Everybody was complimenting the bride on how beautiful she looked. She linked arms with the groom. Her smiling face was radiant, glowing. She leaned against the groom and placed her head on his shoulder.

For this special occasion, the groom had taken off his black shaded spectacles and put on a pair of fashionable designer sunglasses. Donning an all-white groom's suit, he stood tall, motionless, and erect as Jing leaned on him or buzzed around him. He was giving off cool vibes. But I think he was actually feeling quite nervous, because I caught his cheek muscles twitching.

Once his relatives and friends arrived at the banquet hall, he began to relax a bit. His facial muscles no longer twitched. The guests surrounded the young couple and tried to tease the groom. "You look absolutely handsome and dashing today!" they exclaimed.

"Thank you, everyone. You're all so kind."

"Look at your gorgeous bride. The way she carries herself in that gown, she shines brighter than those star celebrities!"

"I may not know what star celebrities look like. But to me, she is the most beautiful."

"Standing side by side, the two of you look like a perfect match."

"We are happy and grateful for your compliments." The groom smiled gently as he spoke.

It was hard to tell what was going on in the guy's head because his facial expression rarely changed. Perhaps being unable to see things was not a real disadvantage. Maybe one day in the future, when Jing's face accidentally gave away sadness or irritation, he wouldn't be able to pick that up. It may not be such a bad thing for married couples, I figured.

An elderly couple slowly ambled toward my side of the room. They wiped tears off their faces as they glanced back toward the white-suited groom standing in the center of the crowd. I think they were probably his parents.

I overheard the groom's mom whispering while sobbing, "I don't know if our decision was a good one or not. I never thought he would get married. I was prepared to take care of him for the rest of his life."

The groom's dad replied, "How can he, a grown man, not want to get married? And even if he's not completely happy in his marriage, it's still an important life experience to have. At least he'll have learned what it's like to be unhappy. Yesterday, I had a really good sit-down chat with Jing. She has thought things through clearly. She knows what she wants. She knows what path she has chosen, and why she chose it. I think she's very honest and genuine. And since he has decided to get married, Jing is a great match for him."

The wedding officiant stepped onto the podium. The room gradually quieted down. Suddenly, the groom called out, "Mom? Where's my mom?" That old woman who had been weeping in the corner of the room walked back toward him and held his hand.

"Mom, please don't leave me today. Don't go anywhere." Their hands were glued together for the rest of the day. Jing stood on the other side of the groom. She kept a joyous smile on her face. In order to have me attend, Jing had taken time off work and personally came to my school to help me apply for a day of absence. I wondered if she was secretly hoping that I would tell Hei Jian all about it later.

Although Jing's new husband could not see the world, he owned a lot of wealth and assets *in* the world. It was said that during his father's generation, their family had already accumulated considerable wealth. The wedding ceremony was grand. Even the heads of the local disability association and the social welfare department were guests. Jing arranged for me to stand right behind the groom. Looking around at the rest of the wedding party, I saw a girl that I've never met before standing behind Jing.

When no one was looking our way, Jing whispered into my ear, "After the ceremony is over, he's going to gift you a red packet."

The groom went to sit in a quieter corner of the room during an intermission in the wedding celebrations, and I was summoned to attend to him.

He squeezed my hand and asked me, "What's your name? Which school are you going to?"

After I had responded to all of his questions, he held out his hand and said, "May I feel you?" I moved a couple of steps closer to him and placed his hand on my head. His fingers were agile. They moved about like the feelers of some type of animal, always alert, vigilant, and on guard. I thought that since he was born blind, his hands must be extra sensitive and swift to fill in for his eyes. "Your bones are nicely proportioned," he told me after he had examined me with his hands. Then, in a mildly anxious tone, he asked, "Could you please take me out of this restaurant? Just outside the door is fine. I'm not very familiar with the layout of this place."

"Where do you want to go?"

"I want to go back to the massage clinic to take a bit of a breather."

"But today, you're the main host of the celebrations."

"There are two main hosts. Only one of us needs to stay," he replied. "Plus, Jing knows where to find me if something comes up."

I walked him out of the hotel restaurant. Once we had exited the front door, I decided to come with. I wanted to check the place out.

The clinic was spotlessly clean, and since it was the owner's wedding day, the room was filled with little gifts for the newlywed couple. All of the presents came from the groom's clients. Moving with grace and ease, the groom walked over to the coffee table, poured himself a cup of water, and sat down. Then he picked up a thick magazine, opened it, and started reading with his index finger.

I stared in awe throughout this whole process. He looked so comfortable and relaxed, moving around like how a person with normal vision would move inside their own home. I remembered Jing telling me that he loved to read. He wrote articles and submitted them for publication in a magazine for the visually impaired.

The clinic was not large, but very cozy. The air was cool and pleasant. There were potted flowers—more than a dozen varieties of them—lining the walls in perfectly staggered layers. The soil inside the shiny, polished flowerpots was soft and moist. The window curtains had a pure white base, upon which floated stalks of dainty, pastel-colored blossoms that swayed gently in the breeze. There was a fish tank in the corner, with a handful of red-headed koi leisurely swimming inside.

After the groom had read a few pages, he said, "Oh!" as if suddenly remembering something. He reached into his pocket, took out a stuffed red envelope, and handed it to me. "You may go now."

"Can I come back here in the future?" I didn't know why, but I was already in love with this place.

"Sure. But what will you do here? You're still so young. You don't need medical massage treatments."

I was quiet for a moment. Then I asked him, "Can only people who are blind learn to perform medical massages?"

"Of course not. My master is not blind. He is one of the most famous Chinese traditional medicine doctors around."

"How many years did you study under him?"

"Oh, quite a few. I can't remember how many exactly. He's actually my uncle, so I've been training with him on and off since I was very young. Of course, I didn't study this every day, because he had to go to work. He only taught me when he was not working."

"Do you plan to have your own apprentices?"

"I don't feel qualified to train any apprentice. I haven't even learned everything there is to know from my uncle yet."

"What if you keep learning from your uncle while you train your own apprentices?"

"Oh, I haven't thought about that. But who would want to apprentice with me?"

"What about me? Can I be your apprentice?"

"But you're still in school! It's much better to go to school and get a proper education. You go from elementary school to middle school to high school, then to college. Follow this path and you will become a very knowledgeable person, with great career potential. What future is there in learning massage therapy? It's one of the vocations that society has given us disabled folks to try to make a living and not go hungry on the streets. You have more options."

How would he know? The kind of future that he was talking about could not have been more distant for me. Besides, it wasn't the kind of path in life I was interested in. I mean, how many people are actually interested in grabbing the moon?

I was becoming warier of hearing people say that I'm resilient, that I can survive the toughest situations, etc. If a kid had an absent mom and a dad who kept playing a game of disappearance—and that kid didn't want to starve to death or kill himself—then they would find ways to stay alive. If you call this "survival skills" and "resilience," then I guess I'm lucky enough to have been given the keys to activating these special powers. I believed that deep inside, everyone had the potential for such powers, but most people just don't get the chance to activate them.

I had already learned from the incident with my aunt that some other powers and potential were lying dormant within me, slowly waking up. And they could take me down a very risky, dangerous path. I didn't want to take that kind of risk, nor become that kind of person. I'm a timid and cowardly guy with no great ambitions. All I wanted was my own warm bed to sleep in and a table to dine on.

I picked up a few of the Braille magazines like the one the groom was reading. I moved my fingers over the columns of tiny dots and asked, "Would you rather have an apprentice who can see or one who is blind?"

"If I were to take on an apprentice, I think I'd probably prefer someone like me. There are many other things a person with full vision can learn. They don't have to come compete with us."

"What if I blinded myself and came back to you? Will you take me on?"

"Good heavens! You scare me." The man sat straight up in his chair. "Who did you say you were? Ah yes, you are one of Jing's guests. What's your relationship to her? How come I've never heard her mention your name? And why do you have those kinds of dark thoughts?"

"I just really like it here, that's all. I fell in love with it the moment I stepped inside."

"I must give Jing a call." Then he dialed a number and held the handset to his ear and waited for a long time. Finally, he let it drop slowly. The wedding banquet was not over yet. With all the guests drinking merrily and chatting rowdily around her, it must have been impossible for Jing to hear the soft ringing of a phone.

"You don't have to call her. If I really wanted to do something to myself, she wouldn't be able to stop me. Maybe she would feel sorry for me. Perhaps other people would also feel sorry for me. But that's just pity. What use is their pity to me? It's only ever helpful to the people feeling the pity. A gentle poke to the heart will make it stronger."

"Heavens!" the groom mumbled. "What are you talking about? Are those words really coming out of a child's mouth?" As he reached out to me with both hands, I quietly stepped back. He let his hands drop.

After a while, he conceded: "Alright, but you do not need to make yourself blind. Not because I think vision is essential to people, but because we should try to preserve the natural order of things. If you were born with fully functional eyes, why damage them? You should try to protect what you have been given, not harm."

My proposal to apprentice at the massage clinic was not well received by Jing. After hearing of it, she didn't say anything at first. She just stuffed her wedding gown into the closet and tore apart her expensive hairdo. Then she shouted angrily at me, "Absolutely not! I don't want you hanging around me every day. I've just started a new life. I don't want it to be tainted by things from the past!"

"If that's how you really felt, then why did you insist on having me attend your wedding ceremony? The truth is, you can't get away from the past. You're just deceiving yourself. Haven't you realized it yet?"

Jing stared at me with gaping eyes. She was wearing mascara and fake eyelashes, so her eyes seemed even bigger than usual. She started to cry. I handed her some paper napkins and she snatched them quickly from me. The fake lashes were really starting to bother her, so she pinched her fingers and gently pulled one of them off. Her eye looked more simple and clean now. She tossed the fake lash into the garbage bin and immediately began reaching for the other side.

After we both calmed down, we decided together that this was what I was going to tell her husband about my background: My dad went to jail; my mom divorced him and got remarried; I had no legal guardian; I had no money to live on; and I was about to drop out of school. As for my relationship with Jing, this was the explanation she came up with: she had planned on adopting me, but the state Children's Welfare and Adoption Center declined her request, saying that my case didn't meet the legal criteria for adoption. So, our relationship fell into that grey zone between potential family members and totally unrelated strangers.

It was a miracle that her husband actually believed us. No wonder Jing said he didn't have a mean bone in him. He was so trusting. And, most of the time, he was content to just hang around family. He had even told her before, "This world is too complicated. I'm glad I don't have to go out very often."

Jing told me more: "Clients who come to him for massage treatment also talk about their own lives and worldly experiences. Over the years, the more he's heard, the less he's wanted to venture out."

As for our complicated past, I promised Jing that I would never bring a hint of it into her new home. I wouldn't dream of doing that. Our past was sealed inside a locked box. Nobody else held the keys to that box, except Hei Jian. And none of us knew where he was. Even if he were to find it in his heart to turn back and look for me, he wouldn't be able to find me. Jing had already moved homes, changed jobs, and gotten a new cell number. If he couldn't find Jing, he wouldn't be able to track me down either. Plus, I don't think it would ever cross his mind that I would be staying with Jing and her husband.

I was determined to work hard and pick up the skills of the trade as quickly as possible. Once I had gained those skills, I planned to leave here and apply for jobs in massage clinics all across the country. Of course, I might have to pretend to be blind, because people who come to massage clinics tend to put more trust in the skills of those therapists.

It would be quite the bold move. Armed with the top-secret skills of massage therapy, I could freely cross between the realms of light and dark, coming and going as I please. What an exhilarating adventure that would be!

Maybe one day I would meet a client who spoke in a familiar voice with a recognizable accent. His head of long, sleek hair would have turned a bit bald in the crown area. His body would be muscular and well-proportioned. Although he was starting to grow a beer belly, he would still move about with brisk, youthful vigor. I would casually ask him questions as I performed the massage. Questions about his kids, lovers, favorite movies, and so on. Caught off guard, he would suddenly lift his head up and stare at me. "You look kind of familiar . . . Do I know you from somewhere? Have us guys met before?"

Of course, he would be correct.

I was barely twelve years old when he left me. And for a young man, those preteen years would become a dividing line between the past and the future—when all that he had known about life was overturned and rewritten.

This scene played out in my head like a poorly-scripted movie, with an awkwardly cliched plot and filmed by a novice director. Of course, the more probable and realistic thing was that our paths would never cross, that Hei Jian and I would never see or hear from each other again.

Now back to that imaginary scene: Every evening, I would return home from the massage clinic after a hard day's work, and my only pastime would be watching movies. I would hunt down and watch nearly every new movie that came out. When the movie finished, I would keep my eyes glued to the screen as the end credits rolled. I would scour the production list for someone named Hei Jian.

But, until the final moments of my life, I would never see his name appear on screen.

Hopefully it was just my imagination.

## ☂ Chapter 15

### I Thought I Would Feel Melancholic
### with Wind and Rain

With the whirling wind and the drizzling rain, I thought I would feel melancholic. But instead, I was feeling restless and excited beyond measure. It was Friday afternoon. I had already packed up the stuff I would need for the weekend. As I sat in class, I checked the clock on the wall impatiently. There was still a long while to go before fifth period—the last class of the day. Time was crawling so slowly.

Today was going to be a historic milestone in my life. After classes were over, I rushed out of the classroom and dashed toward the bus terminal. I was taking the bus to Jiatai's Massage Clinic. Jiatai is the name of Jing's new husband. It also happened to be the name of his massage clinic. Jing and Jiatai had discussed and decided together that I shouldn't quit school to become an apprentice at the clinic. I should use my weekends and holidays to apprentice, just like how Jiatai had apprenticed under his uncle when he was younger.

Back in the day, Jiatai hadn't been the most focused or hardworking apprentice—he would train for a few days, then take the other days off. (As the old saying goes, he fished for three days and hung the net to dry for two.) But Jiatai said that looking back now, it was actually a nice way to learn, because if you're too serious about something and you try to work on it all the time, you can burn yourself out easily and lose your passion.

Earlier that day, when I was still sitting in class, I kept thinking about how I was going to start working and providing for myself like a grown-up. The thought made me giddy with pride. And the closer we got to the end of the school day, the more excited I became. It was like there was a little bunny hopping up and down inside my chest.

I rehearsed over and over in my head the stuff I was going to say to the people I would meet at Jiatai's clinic. "Hello, nice to meet you!" "Thank you for having me!" "My name is Bai Jian. Please take care of me." "Thank you for letting me learn from you." . . . And so on.

And I kept checking my fingernails. I had just recently trimmed my nails. No fleshy thorns were poking out around the nail bed, and no dirt was collecting under the nail edges. In my mind, a person who performs massages for a living should always keep his hands clean and well-sanitized.

Jing was already waiting for me at the entrance to the clinic. She pulled me in front of her and introduced me to every massage master in the place. Then she declared that from now on, I would be coming here on the weekends to help them clean up the place. *What?*

"Not what you expected, right? You know, all apprentices start out like that. First they make tea, clean up, and run errands for their masters. Then, they start to learn their trade," Jing explained. "Those are the accepted rules of apprenticeship."

After she finished, Jing quickly pulled me aside and added in a whisper, "Right now is not the best time for you to start your training. You just need a reason to come here for the weekend." Then she guided me toward a corner of the clinic and showed me a tiny room tucked behind a well-hidden curtain. Inside was a narrow wooden bed and two large storage boxes.

Standing near the end of the bed, Jing pointed to the boxes. "These are for you to store your clothes, toiletries, and other stuff. It's also your study desk. I've tested it out—there's enough space to fit a large workbook on it."

Although I was supposed to help clean up the place, there actually didn't turn out to be much cleaning to do. The floor was shiny and polished. The simple furniture already looked spotless. Everything in the clinic was neatly organized and clean. I looked around the place for a bit, then decided to stand next to Jiatai and watch him do his massage treatments. While observing his movements, I realized that massage therapy was actually very physically demanding work. With each movement he made, the tendons and veins on the back of his hands would bulge and roll. His lips were taut and I saw sweat beading up on the tip of his nose.

At half past ten, Jing forced me to go to bed. There was a slight problem though. In a short while, once everyone had finished their work for the day, they would all head home and leave me stranded here by myself. As if able to read my mind, Jing reassured me that at night the staff took turns staying behind to guard the clinic. They would sleep near the front reception area. If I wanted to, I could lie down in bed and chitchat with whomever was on duty until I fell asleep, since my bed was set up less than three yards from the reception area.

The person on watch duty tonight was a thin, lanky man. He told me that he started to lose his vision later in life, and that he wasn't completely blind. He could still sense light. After the last client of the day had left, he sighed a long sigh and began to roll out his bedding and blanket. I faked a cough, to signal that I wasn't asleep yet. As I expected, he came over.

"This is nice, we can keep each other company tonight," he said. "I'm a bit curious—what's your relationship to Jing?"

"We're not related."

"How can that be? If you're not related to her, then why is she so nice to you? Are you her son?" He smiled coyly. His smile made me feel very uneasy. I stared at his face and wondered whether he could see more than he was letting on: his eyes looked exactly the same as people with normal vision.

Suddenly, I wanted to scare him a little, so that he wouldn't go around gossiping about us. "Tomorrow, I'm going to tell Jing what you just said to me."

"Oh, no, no, no. Don't do that. I was just teasing you. It's a joke. Plus, I'm not the only one here who is suspicious. Jing told all the clinic staff that even when you're around, we are not supposed to slack off. Whatever we were responsible for cleaning before, we should continue to do that. Why would the wife of our boss be so protective of you, a new apprentice?"

"Maybe, as the boss's wife, she just doesn't want you guys to become too lazy and complacent?" I tried to come up with a good explanation to ease his doubts.

"Oh, that may very well be the case. You know her quite well."

The conversation bothered me the more I thought about it. If I were to stay here every weekend, over time, the folks working here were bound to sense something between us. I would be bringing more trouble to Jing. I didn't want to disturb her life and destroy her hard-earned peace. I wanted to run away, to escape from all this. But then I thought, didn't I come here to learn? How could I quit before I even got started? No, I must keep going. Somehow.

I had this ominous feeling that something big and terrible was about to happen. It was like the calm before a storm. Thunder rumbled on the distant edge of the sky; a cool breeze swirled up from the ground, carrying the smell of cold, wet earth.

The very next week, my head teacher approached me and asked about Hei Jian again. "Hey, Bai Jian, when was the last time you had contact with your dad?"

"About three months ago," I answered truthfully.

"So that means he only came to visit you once this entire semester?" She frowned. "Why doesn't he come more often?"

"It's because he's busy shooting movies. Until a movie finishes shooting, the film crew are not allowed to leave the set."

"Is that true? Can you give me his number? I just want to confirm things with him."

"I don't have his number." I lowered my head.

"Have you ever thought that perhaps he is doing this on purpose?" she suggested. "That he wants to abandon his parental responsibilities and just leave you here with us?"

"Nope. He won't do that." I was adamant. "He will come and see me, for sure!"

"No, what I mean is . . . perhaps, just maybe, if something like that were to happen . . . what would you do?"

"I'm going to work a part-time job while going to school, and try to earn the school fees myself. In fact, I have already started to work on the weekends." I almost told my teacher about Jiatai's Massage Clinic, but I held my tongue before I made a blunder. I was afraid that one day Hei Jian would come to the school when I wasn't around and the teacher would give him the address of the massage clinic. He mustn't know about that place.

"How much can you earn on a weekend?" she countered. "Will that be enough to pay your school fees? You know how our fees are higher than the average school."

I couldn't answer her. I hadn't done the calculations, because I didn't know how much Jing planned on paying me each month.

"Because of your unique situation, I have a suggestion for you. Why don't you transfer to one of the regular public elementary schools?" she coaxed. "Their fees are much cheaper and most kids from working-class families go there. Perhaps then you will be able to earn enough school fees by working part-time. And you will be able to fulfill your dream of becoming self-sufficient."

I replied in my head that that wouldn't be possible. The whole reason I came to this boarding school was not because we had loads of money to spend. It was because we had no home, and Hei Jian had no extra time or energy to look after me. So he'd kind of just ditched me here, in a place that provided me room and board.

But the head teacher seemed to have already made up her mind. She said, "Why don't you think it over some more? I really believe that's the best plan for you. We should all know our own limits and work within it, right? All the other students here come from wealthy families—they have a lot more resources. So, if you're okay with it, we will help you with the school transfer process."

After she finished speaking, she walked away, but then quickly turned back. "Did you know, only half of your fees for this semester were paid for? Hei Jian promised us to pay the other half off within one month, but it's now two months past due."

Then she left. She always wore the most perfectly tailored dress suits, even in winter. I heard that her husband was a high-level bureaucrat in the government and her younger brother was also a top local official. Perhaps it was the family influence.

I saw her stop outside the teachers' office, then head down toward the principal's office. I realized that the school was probably planning on expelling me and that she was only there to give me the message from the top. They were worried that Hei Jian was going to abandon me here, so they had to take action before their worry turned into reality. They had to get rid of me—I was becoming a burden and a liability. What could I do to change the situation I was caught in? Was I going to simply let them have their way and kick me out? I quickly analyzed things.

The first issue was money. If they couldn't get a hold of Hei Jian, they wouldn't be able to collect the rest of my school fees, in which case I wouldn't be able to keep that student ID card hanging around my neck. But I couldn't find Hei Jian even if I tried; I could only wait for him to come find me.

The second issue was housing. If I were to transfer into a regular public elementary school, the financial pressure would be less, but where would I go every night after school? And so I didn't have a good solution for either problem.

I stared long and hard at the doorframe of the principal's office. Our principal was an elderly man with snowy white hair. The first and only time I spoke with him was on Teachers' Day back in September, when all the students and teachers sat together and enjoyed a special meal in the school cafeteria. He sat right next to me and asked me why I looked so thin. I told him that my zodiac sign was a pair of bamboo chopsticks. He patted me on the head and chuckled. Then he remarked on how smart and handsome I was. I rebutted, "Would you still compliment me on my appearance if I wasn't smart?" He looked surprised. Then he laughed some more.

Before leaving the cafeteria, he said, "If you're ever bored and don't have anything going on after class, feel free to drop by my office for a chat." But I hadn't had the chance to do that yet.

Perhaps now was a good time to go talk with him.

I fixed my hair and smoothed out the wrinkles on my clothes. I walked up to the door and knocked twice. A voice rose up from inside, "Come in please."

At first, he didn't seem to recognize me, so I reminded him about our shared meal in the cafeteria. He chuckled, "Now I remember. You're the one born under the sign of chopsticks."

I told him that today, I wasn't there to laugh and banter with him. I had important matters to discuss.

For some reason, I didn't feel nervous at all in his presence. I started by introducing myself. As soon as I mentioned my name, he nodded his head. So, he must have already heard Bai Jian's story. He just wasn't aware that Bai Jian was the "chopsticks sign" kid he had met before. This was good. It saved me from having to explain everything in detail. So I told him straight up what I wanted.

I needed the school to give me more time. If Hei Jian hadn't returned before the end of the semester and settled my fees in full, then I would voluntarily leave. As for the unpaid fees, I would write them a loan slip and do my best to repay everything in the future.

"Will you trust me?" I asked. "And please don't misunderstand my dad. He must have been caught up in something out of his control. He will never abandon me though. I was already abandoned by my mom once, back when I was just eight months old. He knows that, so no matter what happens, he will never put me through something like that again. He told me so himself. And if he really wanted to get rid of me, he would have done it a long time ago, instead of waiting until now."

The principal gazed at me when I finished, silent and motionless. And I gazed at him. Deep in my heart, I pleaded, *Please say something? Don't just stare at me. Let me know your decision.*

He cleared his throat, rubbed his chin, and sagged his shoulders. "I have to agree to your proposal. Because you are such an expert negotiator, you leave me no other options. You also make me feel so ashamed as an educator. I never knew that in my school there was a student living under such difficult circumstances."

"Yay!" I nearly jumped with joy. To express my gratitude, I said, "Do you want to hear another joke today? I've got some good ones."

He stood up solemnly and gently shook his head. "I'm not really in the mood for jokes right now, Bai Jian."

But my joy was short-lived. As I left, I began to worry. What if Hei Jian didn't show up before the end of the semester? What would I do then? In three months, what would become of my life?

That weekend, I paid extra attention at Jiatai's Massage Clinic. I watched the masters' every move and carefully imitated them. Perhaps in three months, this place would become my home.

But somehow, Jiatai discovered my plan. I was beginning to think that even when someone cannot physically see the world with their eyes, they aren't any less perceptive.

After sending away another client, Jiatai pulled me aside and asked, "Are you really this passionate about learning massage therapy?"

I couldn't answer him. I hadn't considered it before in terms of passion or liking.

"A person has to have ambition and long-term goals. You can't just focus on the tiny space right in front of you," he said.

"What if I told you that I can't even afford to pay off my school fees? That I'm about to get expelled? Do you still think I should dream high and have tall ambitions? If you allow me to stay here and learn some skills, I can at least feed myself one day and not starve to death. I think that's the best I can hope for right now."

"That's a very short-sighted way to live. Really, you should be reaching for something that's distant and lofty, not what's already before your feet. That's not a goal. It's an excuse—an excuse to stop trying."

I stared at him with surprise and awe.

"Give up your lazy little excuse. Let me offer you a suggestion. Why don't you write a loan slip? I will loan you the money you need. On the slip, you can specify how much money you want to borrow. My only condition is, when you graduate from college and begin to earn on your own, you must repay me double the amount you borrowed. Do you agree to that?"

"What if I can't even get into college?"

"Then you must pay me back five times the loan amount."

I leaped up and gave him a giant hug. He was a tall, muscular, heavy-set guy. His torso was much more sturdy than Hei Jian's.

"Why are you trying to help me, Jiatai?"

"Because of Jing. She adores you. And I love her."

## ☐ Chapter 16

The City was Quiet and Peaceful at the Break of Dawn

The city was so quiet and peaceful at the break of dawn. I had never gotten up this early before. If it wasn't for that one thing that kept me awake, I would still be deep in slumber.

I think that life is strung together by countless problems. Just when I'd managed to solve one problem, that of getting expelled from school, other problems cropped up. I was completely isolated now from my classmates. They didn't want to hang out with me anymore. Whenever I started to talk about something, they would ignore me and pretend like I wasn't there. They refused to let me join in their basketball games. Even in the cafeteria, they would stay far away from me when queueing up for food or eating, and they kept checking their pockets to see if their precious belongings were still there.

It was all my aunt's fault. She'd labelled me a "three-handed thief" when she stormed in here the other day. Who would want to be friends with a three-handed thief?

I realized that nobody in this world can truly help you. Even if someone is willing to help, it's still up to you to show them how to do it. And if you do nothing, the problem will grow bigger and bigger until it swallows you up whole. I had learned this from personal experience.

So I told myself that I must come up with a strategy. I had to change the situation around me somehow, and quickly. Otherwise, I might as well drop out of school.

I stayed up for almost an entire night. I spent the first half of the night thinking hard. Then, during the second half of the night, I composed a confession letter.

First, let me summarize the stuff I was thinking about:

My mind had been very busy and distracted these past few days. I had no clue where Hei Jian was, or whether he was even alive anymore. For all I knew, he could have been involved in an accident or something like that. And if he was alive, why hadn't he contacted me yet? Why didn't he give me his new cell number? All he had to do was call me up and tell me the number. It would have only taken him a minute. Didn't he have even one minute to spare? Or was I not even worth one minute of his time? In fact, it may not even take one minute. He could just make a call when he went to the bathroom. He had often sat on the toilet, chatting away on his phone. I've seen him.

But if he had truly gotten into some kind of accident that would be the most disastrous scenario. From what I knew of Hei Jian, he never carried anything on him that could prove my relationship to him. He didn't even let me call him "Dad." I think he just didn't want other people to know that I'm his son. He wanted to keep up the appearance of being single and celibate.

I couldn't bear to imagine what would happen if he was badly injured in an accident. No one would be able to contact me and let me know. We might not even have the chance to say our final goodbye, before being permanently torn apart by death. . . . My heart was filled with sadness and fear.

Then there was the problem of my aunt. After she had blown up at me in the school cafeteria, she'd just walked off. She hadn't even thought about how much her words and actions would affect me in the future. Or maybe that was her intention. Perhaps that's why she had stormed into my school at lunchtime that day? But I hadn't spent any of the money in that box, not even one cent. I just took her little box on a short excursion to school. She didn't end up losing anything from it, but that wasn't the case for me. I was hurting and suffering greatly. My situation was becoming more and more dire.

During the second half of that sleepless night, I finally came up with the idea. I would write some kind of confessional and post it on the school bulletin board for everyone to see. That way people could read it and know the truth, and judge for themselves.

I climbed off my bed quietly, grabbed a pencil and a piece of paper, and snuck out of the dorm room. Leaning forward against a wall, I spread out the piece of paper and began scribbling.

### *My Confession Letter*

*I swear to the heavens that every sentence I write below is the God-honest truth. The whole truth, and nothing less.*

*For the last few days, I have been seriously reflecting on my past actions. I know I have made some major mistakes.*

*First, I used dishonest methods to collect money for my school fees this semester. I had obtained that money from two separate sources. The first source is Jie. Jie is my birth mother, but she never took care of me. She abandoned me when I was just eight months old. When I went to ask her for the money, I thought she owed me that money. It was the first time in my life that I had asked her for anything. But I didn't end up using that money to pay off my school fees. My dad Hei Jian was really sick, so I gave the money to him, so he could go see a doctor and get medical treatment. I think he might have used that money to buy himself a train ticket out of town, because he disappeared the same day I handed him the money and I haven't heard from him since then. The second source of money was my old aunt. After my grandma had passed away, my aunt had a big falling out with my dad. She kicked us out of my nainai's house and took possession of our family property. She told us that Nainai had passed on that property to her in the will, but Hei Jian said that my aunt tampered with Nainai's will and stole the house from us.*

*So, this is my confession: I have done a few things wrong in the process of trying to get money for my school fees. First of all, I shouldn't have openly blamed my mom for abandoning me. She must have had her reasons when she made this decision years ago. And when she handed me the money, she was crying. I think what I said to her must have really hurt her feelings. As for my aunt, I shouldn't have lied to her saying that I had dreamt of Nainai. I had told her that Nainai was the one who had sent me to her to ask for money. I shouldn't have used Nainai's name in such a disrespectful, deceitful way.*

*The second major mistake I made was that I removed a small metal box containing my aunt's weekly grocery money from her kitchen. Ever since I was little, my dad has been telling me that my aunt is our enemy; that she is the reason that we became homeless. But I'm not here to judge anyone, or to debate whether my aunt or my dad is right. I just want to examine my own actions.*

*Even if my aunt was our worst enemy, or the most wicked person in the world, that doesn't excuse me for stealing from her. Although I never spent a single cent from that box, the moment I reached for it, I had already committed a crime.*

*No matter what my motivations were, it's never right to steal someone else's money. Otherwise, every thief in the world could find an excuse for their actions.*

*The reason I'm writing all this down is because I want you to know the truth and because I need your help keeping me accountable as I try to correct these mistakes.*

*My next step is to write Jie a loan receipt for the money that she gave me. I must give her that receipt whether or not she decides to accept it. After all, love is more about giving than asking or receiving. When I grow up and start to earn money, I will come back and pay her the full amount that I owe.*

*As for my aunt, I'm still at a loss for what to do. According to Nainai's will, my aunt also has the responsibility of taking care of me. So far, she hasn't held up her side of the bargain. Perhaps she has had her share of challenges too. After she and her family had that big argument with Hei Jian, he forbade her from coming near me. So, I want to use this opportunity to ask all of you for advice. This is my question: Should I force my aunt to perform her caregiver duties, or should I let things slide? Ultimately, I'm still hoping to repair my relationship with my aunt. I want to be back on good terms with her even though it might be very difficult—if not impossible—after everything that has happened.*

*When I first came up with the idea of writing a confession letter, my heart was very conflicted. For the longest time, I have tried to cover up my background and living situation from all of you. I didn't want people to know that my family is broke. I didn't want to tell people that my dad has no real job and that we own no property or other valuable assets. We have no roof over our heads, no kitchen to eat in, and no furniture or appliances. And I have no mom. But now, after I made myself put it all down, my heart feels calm and peaceful. I suddenly realize that poverty is nothing shameful or embarrassing. It's not a crime to be poor, but it's also not a good excuse to become corrupt and lose one's dignity and self-respect. If someone tries to change their fortune by using underhanded methods, then they have let poverty become their shame.*

## Epilogue

I posted my confession letter on the school's public announcement bulletin board, then went back to try to catch some sleep. I slept very soundly after that. When my morning alarm rang, I thought it was a bell ringing inside my dreams.

And for a little while, I kind of just forgot about the whole thing. When I tried to go back and check the bulletin board later, the letter that I had posted was gone. I didn't know what had happened. Did it get swept away by the wind or torn off by someone?

On Thursday afternoon, during our weekly class meeting, our head teacher announced out of the blue, "For today's meeting, we will be sharing our thoughts on Bai Jian's confession letter. I assigned this topic as your homework earlier in the week. Now, let's move on to the discussions."

I was shocked beyond belief. Suddenly, I felt like I was sitting on pins and needles.

All of my classmates were eager to speak. The mood of the discussion was energetic and lively. One person gave the opinion that I didn't need to write up a loan receipt because I was still an underaged person—a child. And, as children, we and our actions are legally considered the responsibility of our parents and guardians. Another classmate said that the money my mom gave me shouldn't be counted as a loan. "She's your mom. She should have given you your school money voluntarily. Plus, even if it is considered a loan, the debtor should be Hei Jian because he's the person that spent the money."

Someone else commented that my aunt's actions were very devious: "She exploited the kindness of a sick, elderly person. What she did was no better than robbery."

Another student held a different view: "No matter what underhanded methods she used, her actions are ultimately protected by the law."

Toward the end of the meeting, a girl walked up to the podium. Blushing, she said, "I have a proposal. I think each of us should take turns inviting Bai Jian to our homes for the weekend. What does everyone think?"

"Yes. Agreed!" There was a strong wave of approval rising all around me. I stood up amid my classmates' loud cheers and applause. I hadn't thought things would turn out this way. My mind went blank. I was totally lost for words.

The head teacher said to me, "You are so courageous, Bai Jian. You have overcome the fears in your heart to admit to your own mistakes. We should all learn from you. Plus, by being honest, you are giving yourself a self-healing session—it's therapeutic to be able to unburden your mind, isn't it? When you put those personal shadows into words, they no longer hold as much power over you. Otherwise, the shadows may keep following you for the rest of your life."

"Does anyone want to come with me to deliver the loan receipt to my mom?" I wasn't even sure why I was doing this.

Everybody in class raised their hands. But in the end, the class decided that our class rep would go with me. I took my confession letter and a loan receipt and then off we went.

As we walked together, the class rep kept telling me, "You know, it really isn't necessary to give that loan receipt to your mom. The money she gave you shouldn't count as a loan. It's her job as a parent to put you through school."

"What you're talking about is what happens under normal situations. My situation is kind of different. My mom was an unwed mom when she gave birth to me, so I don't even have a valid permanent residence registration certificate. I don't know if unmarried parents have the same legal duty of care toward their children."

I saw his eyes widen with surprise and his feet briefly stop in their tracks.

Before today, I had always avoided talking about such personal matters, but now, I didn't care anymore. The fact that I dared to speak about these things meant I was no longer tormented by them. I no longer saw them as the source of pain and shame. And honestly, they really shouldn't be. Just like how a person cannot change their genetic makeup, they cannot be held responsible for the things that she or he was born with—the stuff beyond their control. It was as simple as that.

When we arrived at Jie's place, she was munching on a piece of cucumber. Her appearance surprised me. Her belly was round and bulging, but her face looked thin and sunken. When she saw me, she broke into a smile. "Guess what, you are going to have a baby sister soon. Or maybe it's a baby brother. What do you think? Is it a boy or a girl?"

"I don't know." I handed her my confession letter and the loan receipt.

She read them over quickly. "What's this? A confession? Did you write it? Who told you to write it? What is it for?" Then she looked at the loan receipt and added: "If I knew you were going to give him the money, I wouldn't have lent it to you." After saying that, she carefully folded those papers and tucked them into her pocket.

"Can I please have my confession letter back?" I asked politely. "I still need to use it."

She took it out slowly, and hesitated before giving it back to me. "Hey, Bai Jian, why don't you write a disclaimer on the loan receipt saying that you borrowed the money for Hei Jian? I don't need you to pay back the money. But since he took that money and spent it, I may go after him in the future."

Before we left, she asked us to wait there for a moment. She shuffled into a backroom and soon re-emerged with a plastic bag in hand. She gave me the bag. I opened it and peeked inside. Within were a bunch of clothes that she had bought for me, as well as some snacks.

After doing a lot of thinking, I decided not to visit my aunt's place that day because I hadn't come up with a good plan yet. The class rep agreed with me. We figured we should probably go back and ask the class for more advice.

On Friday morning, the class rep handed me a sheet with the schedule of who was going to be hosting me each weekend, starting that very week. For the first weekend, I was going to the class rep's home. Then I would go to the next person on the list the following weekend, and so on. This arrangement would continue until the last week of the semester.

But I had other plans in mind. Two days ago, I had secretly celebrated my twelfth birthday on my own. The way I celebrated it was quite unique, I thought: I spent one yuan having my height and weight taken at the community health center across the street from my school.

Height: 166 cm, Weight: 48.5 kg

Those were not the body measurements of a child, which meant I was entering adolescence. It was time to wave goodbye to my childhood.

And in a sense, I was ready to make some big decisions about my future. For example, did I wish to become a fearless eagle that would pierce through clouds and conquer the sky? Or was I content being a lazy, cowardly sparrow that only begged to be fed for the day?

I agreed with what Jiatai had said. I would no longer go to the massage clinic on the weekends or waste my time idling around. At school, my principal started to drop by often to check in on me. After some more open and friendly discussions with him, I decided to form a weekend peer-study group. Everyone who wished to participate was welcome.

On Saturday or Sunday morning, we would gather at school to complete our homework together. As we worked through the problems, we would each write down the items we had trouble solving. Next, we would draw up a list of these difficult items and put our heads together to tackle them one by one. If nobody knew the answer to a question, then we would bring that item to our teacher. Oh, and another thing: Our principal assigned one teacher to be on shift every weekend to supervise and help us. This teacher would join our homework discussions during the day, and sleep in the student dorm at night to keep me company.

It was decided that any new problem or challenge that came up in my life was no longer mine alone. They were to be considered the responsibility of the school. My principal said that things like that shouldn't be put on individuals like Jing or Jiatai or any of the other students to find a solution to. The solution should come from within the institution—it was the school's job to help me succeed.

On the tenth weekend of our peer-study program—or, to be more exact, on the ninety-ninth day after I turned twelve—Hei Jian finally called.

His voice blasted out through the speaker: "My boy, right now you're taking an *international long-distance* call. We're in Ukraine this month filming a snow scene. The scenery here is unreal! Once the movie comes out in theaters, you'll be able to see it too."

I asked him the question I had been waiting to all this time. "I read the news article about your film crew's visit to our city. I've also seen photos of the set that people took. How come I've never seen you in any of them?"

Hei Jian chuckled. "Don't you understand? While other people were idling around getting interviewed, I was keeping myself busy with work. How are things going with you?"

"Great. And you?"

"Great."

The two of us burst into laughter together.

Hei Jian said that once he had finished shooting this movie, he would come visit me. He said that he loved his job so much he would do it in a heartbeat, even if nobody paid him a cent.

"You'd still do it even if it took you away from your own son. Right?" I added.

"You know me the best!"

We laughed again.

"Hey baby boy, I miss you a lot!"

"Oh, *COME ON*. Get back to your work!"

I heard him cracking up on the other side of the line. With the sound of his laughter still fresh in my ears, I hung up the phone.

I was smiling too.

## THE END

# *About the Author*

**Yao Emei** is an author of books for both children and adults who has won awards such as the People's Literature award, the Selection of Novella award, and the Shanghai Literature Excellent Novella Award. Her books have been translated from Chinese into English, Russian, German, Japanese, Korean, and other languages. *Tilted Sky* is her first children's book to be translated into English. She lives in Shanghai.

# *About the Translator*

**Kelly Zhang** is a first-generation Chinese immigrant, bilingual author, and literary translator based in Ottawa, Canada. She writes heartfelt stories inspired by her heritage culture and informed by her lived experiences. Kelly also translates contemporary children's fiction originating from mainland China and the Chinese diaspora, and always seeks to elevate the voices of young emerging writers and women creatives. Her debut picture book as writer, *Take Me to Laolao*, and as translator, *Grandma's Roof Garden*, are forthcoming in 2024 from Quill Tree and Levine Querido respectively. Connect with Kelly on Twitter (@Kelly Zhang_YL) or visit her website: www.kellyzhangyl.com.